OH WHAT FUN

Emily Slate Mystery Thriller Holiday Special

ALEX SIGMORE

Dark Woods Press

OH WHAT FUN: EMILY SLATE MYSTERY THRILLER HOLIDAY SPECIAL

1st Edition

ebook ISBN 978-1-957536-43-9

Print ISBN 978-1-957536-44-6

Description

Not all is Merry and Bright.

While it may be a festive season for most, for Special Agent Emily Slate, Christmas is nothing more than a nuisance—a time when crowds and traffic get worse, and tempers run hotter.

As if Emily didn't have enough trouble surviving the season unscathed, a recent string of robberies has just turned deadly. A trio of robbers, each dressed as Santa Claus, have been looting local jewelry stores and their most recent attack has claimed the life of a young woman.

Determined to stop the thieves before they escalate further, Emily and Zara take the case, using their wits and skills to track down the robbers before they can strike again.

But this is no average holiday heist. Dark and twisted motives have put this plan into motion and Emily will find herself feeling the whiplash as she attempts to navigate the twists and turns of this unique case.

If these criminals aren't caught before holiday is over, there's no telling how much carnage they may leave in their wake.

Chapter One

"UGH, THIS IS THE WORST."

My best friend and fellow FBI Agent Zara Foley turns to me, her eyes wide and accusing, as if I've just slaughtered a baby lamb. "Are you kidding? This is *the best*!"

All around us are smiling faces, people happily going about their day. Festive music plays over the sound system while everything in the mall is decorated in some variation of red, gold, or green. It's an onslaught to the senses and there are just so. Many. People.

"Why did I let you drag me here?" I ask as a child going to town on some kind of sucker passes us, holding the hand of their parent. She looks up at me and I can't help but shy away. Damn, I thought I was getting better about that.

"Because you need something for your new boyfriend and given your taste in gifts, you need my help not to scare him off before this thing has even gotten off the ground," she says, scanning the storefronts.

I've been an FBI agent for almost five years now, been through more harrowing situations than I enjoy thinking about. Despite facing some of the darkest and most twisted sickos out there, here I am, in a normal American mall in the middle of December, freaking out about being stuck in the holiday season.

I'm not a Christmas person. Never have been. I *used* to be, back when it was me and Mom and Dad. But after Mom died it seemed like the holiday died with her. Dad tried his best to make things fun, but without her it took the wind out of my sails, and for a long time I didn't even want to acknowledge the holiday. It was only after I met Matt that I finally opened up a little and started celebrating again.

"C'mon, you have to admit this is just a little bit *fun*," Zara says, practically skipping along as we make our way through the mall. "Look at everyone, they're all full of holiday spirit and joy. Just think about the families going back home to bake cookies and watch movies and stay up all night drinking egg nog."

I eye her suspiciously. "Did you sniff something from the evidence locker before we got here? That stuff doesn't happen in real life, it's reserved for crappy holiday movies on greeting card channels."

"Fine, be a grump," she replies. "I'll refrain from calling you the other "G" word just because I'm afraid you might try to pistol whip me." She grins then breaks out into a laugh as she says it. Man, she is *wired*. Usually Zara is a lot more upbeat and bubbly than I am, but this is another level. Before Matt died, she and I were friends, but we never spent as much time together as we do now. So I never really saw her around the holidays—at least, not like this.

"Let's just find something and get out of here as fast as humanly possible, please?" I suggest.

"If you keep complaining, I'm going to sit you down and make you watch the animatronic bear show at the end of the mall," she chides.

"Animatronic bear show?" I ask.

"Sure, it's a mall staple. They've had it for years. I remember seeing it when I was a kid," she says.

"What the hell is it?"

"Just what it sounds like. About twenty animatronic bears, all dressed to the nines, and all playing different instruments in a classical orchestra setting. You know, violins, trumpets, flutes…there's even one on a piano."

"And they…*play* the instruments?"

"Well, I mean they move choreographed to a soundtrack so it *looks like* they're playing the instruments," she says. "But really, they're just moving along to the music. Though little kids can't tell."

"That sounds like the stupidest thing I've ever heard," I say.

Her eyes go wide. "Oh, then we *have* to see it." She grabs the lapel of my jacket, attempting to pull me along.

"How are you so energized? Didn't your legs get torn up like two weeks ago?" I ask, referring to the injury she sustained when we were both up in Vermont. She'd been tangled up in some barbed wire as we'd been chasing a suspect. And while the injuries hadn't been serious, they'd drawn a lot of blood.

"It's the human body, Em, it heals," she says, deadpan. "What, are you saying I don't have the strength to get you there? I'm not afraid of a little sparring session right here in the middle of the mall. People would love it."

I know she's just screwing with me, but I can't help but chuckle. "Yeah, that'd go down real well with security."

"Ah, we can take them too," she says, waving me off. "Come on. Bears. Now."

"Can't we at least get a present for Liam first?" I ask, allowing myself to be dragged, though not without making her work for it.

"If you'll hurry up and make up your mind about what you want to get for him," she replies.

"I dunno," I admit. "Matt was so easy to shop for. You could literally buy the man anything and he'd be happy. But Liam…" Not to mention my relationship with Liam is still very…new. We only got together a few months ago, after I almost died when a group called the Organization made it their mission to hunt me down. And not long after that, I received a strange letter written in my mother's handwriting. Through it all, Liam and I have tried to deny our attraction for each other, but it reached a point after I almost died that we both realized pretending our feelings didn't exist was too difficult.

So now, here I am, less than a week before Christmas, trying to find a present for the first man I've felt anything for since my husband died.

"What are you getting Raoul?" I ask, hoping Zara's answer will spur my imagination.

"He likes fancy scents, so he gets a bottle of *Dior Sauvage*." She says it with a French accent, exaggerating her enunciation.

"Maybe I should get that for Liam," I say.

"What kind of cologne does he wear?" she asks.

I give her a sheepish look.

"You don't know?"

"I never looked!" Okay. I'm not much of a perfume girl. I'll spritz some on every once in a blue moon, but it's not something I regularly go for. One, it's not a great impression when heading to a crime scene to pull up smelling like a fifty-dollar hooker. Two, it aggravates my allergies when I wear potent stuff for too long. Deodorant is fine enough for me, as long as I shower regularly.

"What am I going to do with you?" She shakes her head like I've just failed the ultimate chick test. "I think cologne is out. You don't want to buy him something that clashes with his natural scents."

"Right, because that would be a disaster," I say, rolling my eyes as we continue walking down the middle of the mall.

"You joke, but you know how some guys just smell like ass?

That's bad scent matching. It's like putting marinara sauce on sushi. It just isn't going to come out right."

"Or they're just unkempt," I reply.

"Okay, so what does he like? Any favorite movies? I'd say you could get him a tie but—"

"Liam hates ties," I reply.

"—Liam hates ties," she reiterates. He's made it no secret he doesn't enjoy wearing a tie around the office, though he pulls it off quite nicely. In fact, he can rock a suit better than a lot of guys. But on the occasions I've seen him as the day is ending, his tie is the first thing to come off.

"What about liquor?" I say. "Guys love liquor."

"*You* love liquor," she replies. "It's bad form to buy a gift for someone that's really just something you want yourself."

I mean, she's not wrong. I wouldn't say no to a nice tequila or bourbon, but I'm digging at the bottom of the barrel here. "I'm out."

"You're not out. Think about what he likes to do. What is his favorite pastime? What—"

"Oh!" I yell, startling a young family passing by. "He loves soccer. Or…futbol, as he calls it. Loves it."

"Great, what's his favorite team?" When I give her a blank stare, Zara only narrows her gaze at me. "Emily. What is your boyfriend's favorite sports team?"

I grimace. "The…*Cutters*? That's a team, right?"

She starts swatting at me so much that I put my hands up to defend myself. If we weren't making a scene before, we sure are now. "You are so bad at this!"

"I know!" I yell back. "I can't help it!"

Finally, the swatting stops as she steps back, pinching the bridge of her nose. "You are absolutely hopeless."

I give her a sheepish smile. "Maybe I should just give him a gift card or something."

"On your first Christmas together? Is that the memory you want seared into your mind forever?" She straightens, adopting a slightly deeper voice that's a bad impression of me. "Hey, Liam, here you go. I didn't care enough to pay attention to what you liked, so I just figured you could buy yourself something nice." She steps back, glaring at me.

"Very funny. I don't sound like that."

"You don't *not* sound like that."

"I'm reconsidering the sparring session," I say.

"Seriously, Em, don't you know *anything* about him?"

I shrug. "What can I say? We've only been formally dating…what, a month? Not even? And there's been work, and we had to go to Vermont—"

"No excuse," she replies. "What about his family? They would know, right?"

"I've never met his family."

"No time like the present," she says, turning and heading in the opposite direction. "I'll pull his file at the Bureau, and do a reverse lookup. I'll have names and phone numbers within an hour."

I grab her by the arm. "Z, no. You're not going to use federal resources to track down my boyfriend's family. I get the sense there's some tension between them. Which is I think something we have in common."

"Fine," she says, exasperated. "Well, you better figure out something. We're six days and counting. You can't put this off forever."

"What if I could?" I ask. "I could just tell him that I don't do Christmas and not to get me anything."

"And ruin the amazing gift he's already bought for you?" she asks, then realizing what she's said, slaps a hand over her mouth.

"Wait, what do you know?" I ask, narrowing my eyes.

"Nothing," comes the muffled reply.

"No, you have to tell me," I say, pulling her hand away from her mouth. "What did he get me?"

She gives me a pitiful look. "It's really good."

"Aw, dammit," I say, turning away from her and pacing in a circle. "How good?"

She draws her features together, as serious as a funeral. "Amazing."

I let out a long groan. "Why do we have to do this? Can't human beings just get through December without being subjected to the insanity that surrounds this holiday?"

Zara puts her hand on my shoulder. "Sorry Em. Not in the twenty-first century. If I'd had to guess…I'd say you're screwed."

"You're not being much help," I reply.

"I—" Before she can finish, there's the high-pitched sound of breaking glass, followed by a scream.

Zara and I take one look at each other before we take off running.

Chapter Two

It's not difficult to tell where the commotion is coming from; everyone else is running away from the noise. My first thought is mass shooter, which we're not prepared for. I left my weapon locked up in my car and as far as I know Zara isn't armed. The mall has security, but they're not trained to deal with someone brandishing an automatic weapon. As Zara and I head toward the noise, I pray we're not dealing with something on that scale.

But as I pass the panicked faces of the shoppers, I don't see absolute terror, which is encouraging. Zara and I have to hop over some chairs in the middle of the mall to avoid most of the mob of people. I'd tell them to stay calm but I don't know what we're dealing with here, and I'm not about to not tell someone to run for their life if that's what we're facing.

"Em," Zara says, having cleared the next row of chairs. Most of the people are running around the corner to our left and we hook around the outside, trying to squeeze by. People are already yelling and pushing and it becomes a struggle just to get through.

"Move!" I yell. "FBI, get out of the way!"

My announcement only seems to further panic the crowd.

A child trips and falls, having lost the hand of their parent. Against my better judgment I bend down and help the little girl up before a woman in a white coat pushes out through the crowd. "Julie!"

"Is this your mom?" I ask the little girl, who nods emphatically. I make sure they're connected before continuing to make my way through. I'm being smacked by bags, purses, and hard objects as people shove past me, and I've lost Zara somewhere in the crowd.

Finally, the people thin and I hear more glass breaking somewhere up ahead. I *never* leave my weapon in my car, unless I'm off-duty and am making my way into crowded spaces—for the very reason I don't want to panic anyone if they happen to catch sight of it under my jacket. I figured, *hey, I won't need it in there. How much trouble could I get into shopping?* Apparently the goddess of irony is having a field day today.

"Z!" I call out, spotting her emerging from the crowd on the other side. We both exchange a glance as someone in one of the stores across from us cries out. It's a corner unit, a jewelry store. And inside are—I can't believe it at first—three people dressed up like Santa Claus, wielding large clubs and black backpacks.

I take half a second to assess the situation. The Santas are on the taller side, probably men, but it's impossible to tell underneath the bulky outfits. Each one's face is also covered by a white mask that obscures any of their features, and they're all wearing sunglasses and Santa hats. I can't even see the color of their skin. They each stand in different positions in the store, filling their backpacks with jewelry from the broken display cases around them.

"Freeze! FBI!" I yell, but without my weapon or my badge, I don't have much to brandish at them.

Two of the Santas look up, but I can't see their eyes behind the dark glasses. They both take off running, zipping their backpacks and throwing them on their backs as they go.

The third Santa is standing over one of the store associates, who is on the ground next to the broken glass from the cases, shielding her face, as if she's afraid the Santa is going to beat her with the club.

"Get him!" I tell Zara, pointing at the man running closest to her. The other one has passed by me, but I'm more interested in his friend. How long will it take mall security to get here with that mob back there? The jewelry store had to have tripped the silent alarm, right?

Zara is off like a shot after the first Santa, though I see him duck into a side hallway that runs between the stores in the mall. However, I keep my focus on the Santa who is still in the store. The third one will just have to get away. But if I can get this one under control, I'm reasonably sure we can track down the third guy without a problem.

What I don't like, however, is how the Santa is just standing there, black backpack in one hand, club in the other. He's facing me directly and it's like he's waiting for me to make a move. "Put your hands up and drop your weapon," I tell him, using my best command voice. "You are under arrest."

He doesn't move. Only the clerk on the ground glances in my direction. I notice some blood running down her face, maybe from a cut on her head, I can't tell. Whoever these guys are, at least they aren't using guns. But that doesn't mean they're not dangerous.

"Put your hands up!" I yell again. "I'm not going to tell you a third time."

I'm only about ten feet from the Santa, though there is a broken jewelry case that separates us. If he goes right, he'll have to swerve around another case to get out. If he goes left, he's clear, but I'm closer to that side. Either way, I'm approaching slowly, and his options are dwindling by the second.

"Look, there's nowhere to go," I say. "Just put the club

down and drop the bag." Because I can't see his features, I can't read him, or anticipate what he might do. And as far as I can tell, I'm on my own here. Zara is chasing the other perp and mall security hasn't arrived yet. More than likely they're trying to clear the crowd to get here. There's movement in my periphery, but it's low to the ground. Probably from other retail associates who were attacked. The Santa, however, isn't moving. "Look, I'm a federal officer, and I am placing you under arrest."

As I approach he swings his club at me and I have to dodge, though I feel the breeze as it barely misses me. He breaks left, and I try to intercept but he's quick with that club and it slams into my shoulder hard enough to make me cry out. He takes the opportunity to run in the same direction as the first perp, and he's *fast*. Despite the bulky costume, he's got some speed and I find I have to give it everything I have to keep up with him.

The mall has long since cleared out now and a security guard in a dark blue uniform runs at the Santa from the opposite end. He's reaching for something on his belt, but I'm not sure what. I know for sure it isn't a firearm because they don't carry them, but this mall might employ guards who use tasers. "Watch out," I yell. "He's armed with—"

Before I can finish there is a sickening *crack* as the Santa swings the club and it connects with the security guard's head. The Santa barely even slowed down and is still running as the guard falls to the ground. I slow and check the man's pulse to make sure he's still breathing, which, thankfully he is. But he's out cold and I have no doubt he'll have a concussion. I pull out my phone as I resume my pursuit. I quick dial 911. "This is Special Agent Slate with the FBI. I'm in pursuit of a robbery and assault suspect at Arlington Center Mall on the first floor, headed toward the south exit. Requesting any backup. Suspect is wearing a Santa suit with a mask and glasses."

The operator on the other end confirms she'll relay the information to the local police, who she informs me are already on the way. Already I can feel my legs beginning to burn from pushing them so hard. I've been lax in my cardio lately, after my run-in with the Organization I've been "taking it easy" which unfortunately means I've lost a lot of my stamina.

The Santa begins to pull away from me, and I know if he gets outside, he's likely to have a getaway car waiting for him. But instead of heading for the exit, where I can see groups of people through the glass doors, apparently trying to decide if they can come back in the mall or not, the Santa makes a hard left and pushes through a pair of utility doors.

I follow into the corridor, which isn't open to the general public. It's an access hallway for the stores on either side, and it leads to maintenance areas of the mall. The Santa takes another left down another corridor and I struggle to keep up, my breathing hard and ragged. I didn't realize just how out of shape I was.

I turn the corner only to find it empty. It's probably two or three hundred feet long, but the Santa is nowhere to be seen. However, there are doors on each side of the corridor. The ones on the left lead into the different storefronts that run inside the mall. And the ones on the right seem to access different maintenance areas like electrical rooms. I check the first few doors I pass, slowing to a trot. I'm sure he turned down here, which means he had to have ducked into one of these doors, and it would have had to have been one of the close ones. He didn't have time to go anywhere else.

The first door on the left is no good. It's locked. I head to the next one on the right and it's more of the same, the door proclaiming it as the HVAC room, probably for the entire wing of the mall. There's an errant loading cart sitting in the hallway, apparently abandoned by its user sometime earlier in the day. It's long and flat, much too small to be able to hide anyone, but I approach it cautiously anyway. That's when I see the faint outline of a print on the linoleum floor. It's not much, but it looks like a rubber imprint from a shoe. I look for any others and there's another about a stride away. For whatever reason, this floor may have captured a shoe print of our perp.

Careful to avoid the prints, I check the next door on the right, which is open. Cautiously, I open the door all the way, to find it's just an antechamber that leads out to a loading dock on this side of the mall.

"Dammit," I mutter as I step all the way into the antechamber. The loading dock beyond is empty, and one of the doors has been rolled open. It had to have been like that when the perp ran in here; otherwise, I would have heard him roll it up. Still, I remain vigilant as I make my way into the space. I've been on too many raids where some criminal thought they'd try to be slick by hiding instead of taking the obvious exit. But in this case, I'm relatively sure that's what happened. He must have seen all the crowds outside and known he'd have a harder time navigating them to get away, and thus made his way back here. And lucky for him, there had been another way out.

When I reach the rolled-up door, I peer out. There's about a five-foot drop from where the trucks back their trailers up to the loading dock. But the only trailer here tonight is one three bays down, and both that door and the trailer are closed. The loading dock is in a U-shape, with trailers directly across from me that load for the other side of the mall. And the entrance to the loading area is a service road that runs beside general parking. But as I stare down the road, I know he's gone. Even if I could catch up with him, I'm betting that Santa costume was designed to be removed quickly so he could blend in with a crowd. The crowd that's standing right outside every mall exit at the moment.

Sighing, I head back inside.

Chapter Three

"ANYTHING?" I ask as I spot Zara trudging back to the scene of the crime.

"I lost him in a changing room," she says.

Rubbing my sore shoulder and I can't help but wince. It's definitely going to bruise. "A changing room?"

"Yeah, full of Santa costumes," she replies. "He ducked in there and by the time I had searched everywhere, he was gone. It must be where they supply the costumes for the mall Santas. You?"

"Loading dock," I reply. As we both approach the scene, the Fairfax police have already arrived and are making their assessments. I see the security guard the Santa took out still on the ground, but he's at least sitting up and awake while a paramedic tends to him. Another paramedic is working on the jewelry store employee with the blood on her face. It's then when I see something that makes my heart drop. Two EMTs, working on another employee that's behind some of the cases. She's not moving and her eyes aren't open.

"Sorry folks," one of the officers says as we approach. "You'll have to wait outside. This is an active scene."

"We're FBI," I tell him, keeping an eye on the EMTs. "I'm the agent that called it in. What's the situation?"

"There's one that's critical," he says. "Another employee with at least a concussion. And of course the mall security officer. What are the FBI doing here?"

"Shopping," Zara replies. "Or, at least, trying to."

"Our badges and weapons are in the car," I say to the officer. "But we both attempted to pursue the suspects."

He points over his shoulder. "You'll have to make a report with Sergeant Roeske over there." Beyond him stands a tall man with a thick black moustache and a look on his face like he drank sour milk.

"Right," I tell him. "Thanks." As Zara and I make our way over to the sergeant, I take a second to inspect the damage in the jewelry store and to see if I can't get a better look at the other employee. I didn't see her before because she was behind one case on the far side of the store.

Almost every case is smashed, though not everything has been taken. I would have thought the perps would have grabbed everything, but it looks like they only went for the highest-value stuff. That means they cased the store at some point, maybe even multiple times.

I glance up, looking for the video cameras, only to find them embedded in small black half-moons attached to the ceiling. Like the kind they use in Vegas casinos. It allows the cameras to be omnidirectional without drawing any attention to them.

Zara and I stand close to the EMTs, but I can already tell by the way they're moving it's too late. The woman—she looks like she's in her late twenties with dark brown hair and a nice, tailored suit—is lying on the ground between them. A dark pool of blood lies under her, soaking into the carpet.

"Damn," I say.

"You're the FBI agents?" a gruff voice asks as I'm

inspecting all the broken glass scattered all over the floor. I turn to see Roeske and another officer approaching.

"Special Agent Slate. This is Special Agent Foley," I tell him, holding out a hand to shake, but he doesn't take it.

"Let's see your badges," he says.

"They're in our vehicles," I reply. "Along with our service weapons."

He narrows his eyes. "Let me see some ID." I sigh and pull out my wallet, showing him my driver's license. Zara does the same. "You two could just be a couple of adrenaline junkies."

"I've got the FBI logo tattooed on my ass if you'd like to see that," Zara says.

Roeske gives her one of the nastiest looks I've ever seen, though I have to hold my tongue. He turns to his officer. "Call the FBI. Verify these two." The officer nods and heads off, speaking into his radio. Roeske turns back to us. "Assuming you're who you say you are, you'll need to make formal reports."

"We know how this goes," I say.

"I don't suppose you'd like to tell me who did this, given the vast resources of the FBI," he says.

"Three people, likely men, dressed up as Santas," I say. "They were careful not to show any skin or their faces. But I believe there might be a shoe print near the loading dock. Floor looked recently polished. It might have picked up a partial."

"Fine," he replies, though I can tell he's not putting much stock in what we have to say. "Make your statements with Officer Sharpe over there, then you're free to go."

"Gee, thanks," Zara says. As soon as we're out of earshot, she glances back at him. "Watch out for big dick city over there. If he turns around too fast he might knock you over with it."

I can't help but chuckle, despite the dour circumstances. "He's just doing the dominance thing. Probably got freaked out the second he heard feds were on *his* scene. He's got a robbery *and* a murder to deal with."

She adopts a lithe tone. "Why is it all the biggest men are always the most insecure?"

"You got me," I reply. "Let's just make our statement so I can go home. I think I've had enough of the mall for one day."

~

I'M SITTING IN MY NEW BOSS'S OFFICE, WATCHING HIM STARE AT a computer screen while I attempt not to go out of my mind with boredom. Fletcher Wallace has been head of our division for almost a month now, and despite a rocky start, I feel like the two of us are making progress. Though I try not to think too hard about how much he wanted me gone as soon as he took the job.

"Brief report," he finally says.

"There wasn't a lot to tell," I reply. "Agent Foley and I heard the robbery taking place, attempted to stop the perpetrators—"

"But they got away," he replies.

"They did," I say. "But I'd also like to take this time to point out I was *off*-duty at the time."

His gaze flicks from the screen to me and back again before he sits back in what used to be the chair that belonged to my old boss, Janice Simmons. Since her promotion to deputy director I don't see her much anymore, but I feel like even though Janice was never the warmest of people, she'd be more sympathetic about this situation. Zara and I are just coming off a difficult case in Vermont involving the murders of four men. I'm inclined to take some of this time off I've been accruing.

"Sergeant Roeske," Wallace says, his attention back on the screen.

"You know him?" I ask.

"We've crossed paths," he replies. "But it's not important. According to Fairfax police, this is the third robbery of this nature. But it's the first one where there's been a casualty."

"All jewelry stores?" I ask.

He nods. "And all in different malls. Tyson's Corner, Fair Oaks and now Arlington Center. We've got ourselves a pattern."

My ears perk up. "I'm sorry. *We*?"

He turns to me. "I want you on this."

"On a *robbery* case?"

"This is no normal petty theft," he replies. "The thieves have stolen over one *million* dollars worth of jewelry. And they just crossed over into D.C. You have some experience in the fencing arena, don't you? I read that in your file."

"Yeah, about a hundred years ago," I reply. "I investigated fencing operations after my first six months in the Bureau. I'm sure there are more qualified—"

"I don't disagree," he replies. "But everyone else has families they'd like to be with during the holidays. If I'm not mistaken, that's not a problem for you."

His words cut deep, but I don't let my face show the turmoil of emotions he's just unleashed.

"Good. Coordinate with Fairfax. I'm sure Roeske will be more than happy to lend some assistance."

"What about my other cases? I've got at least—"

"Face it, Slate," he says. "You're not going to make any progress on those before the holiday. But if we can shut this thing down before it grows too large, I'll consider that a win."

I take back what I said earlier. Wallace really has this asshole thing down pat. "Fine."

"Good. Looking forward to seeing what you come up with." Without another word I head back to my desk, catching Zara's eye as I sit down. I give her an epic eye roll.

"That bad, huh?"

"He wants me to work the case," I say. "Like I don't already have a hundred better things to do."

"Wait, you're going after the Santa's?" she asks and I can already see the ideas percolating in that brain of hers.

"Why, you want to take over? I'll gladly hand it off to you."

"Of course I want it," she replies. "But we're running this one together. I'm not going to let you Scrooge yourself out of it." She stands and cups her hands over her mouth to simulate a megaphone. "*Hey, Liam!*"

"What are you doing?" I hiss.

My new boyfriend gets up from his desk about twenty feet away and heads over, a big grin on his face. He doesn't take his eyes off me the whole time.

"Okay you two, save it for when you get home," Zara says. "Liam, remember that favor you owe me?"

"Favor?" I ask.

"Oh yeah. Back from that little bet he lost."

I turn to Liam, confusion on my face. He sighs. "Zara bet me that you and I would be together before the end of the year."

"And you didn't think we would?" I ask, a strange, unwelcome sensation creeping up my belly.

"Honestly, I didn't think you'd ever want to make things serious," he replies. "I didn't think you'd want to get into a relationship again so soon. Plus, this was before you almost died from that car wreck and the poison."

"Oh," I say, somewhat relieved. "Yeah, that did kind of change things."

"Anyway, I lost the bet," Liam says.

"And now you gotta pay up," Zara replies.

He shoots me a knowing look before facing his fate. "What's the damage?"

"I need you to cover a couple of cases for me while I help Em catch the Santa robbers."

He shakes his head like he didn't hear her correctly. "I'm sorry. The...*what?*"

"Santa. Robbers," she replies. "What's so hard about that? They're Santas that rob places. And your new girlfriend is on the case."

He turns to me. "Seriously?"

"Wallace just informed me."

"But I, being the good friend that I am, can't let her chase down three potentially murderous jolly ol' elves by herself, can I?" she asks. "So I need you to cover."

"Actually, I think I would feel better with the two of you together," he says. "I wasn't as worried when I knew you had each other's backs up in Vermont."

"You should have seen it," Zara says, suddenly more excited. "I got her to wear this *insanely* short dress. I think I have a picture of it somewhere..." She pulls out her phone and starts scrolling.

I reach over and snatch the phone out of her hand. "Anyway," I say. "It's just a string of robberies. A poor girl was killed in the last one. I don't even know why Wallace wants me on this. It's stuff for the local LEOs."

"I'm sure you'll do great," Liam says. "Though I wouldn't mind seeing that picture one day."

Zara is trying to swipe the phone from my hands, but our desks are between us and she doesn't have the reach. "Maybe," I tell him. "If I'm not mortified."

"It's a good dress," she reiterates, having given up. Then leans in closer to him, conspiratorially. "Don't worry. I'll text it to her."

"And we'll both delete it off our phones," I say.

"Yes. And you *definitely* won't see it anywhere else, ever again. *Especially* not at your wedding when I do the photo collage."

Liam is grinning at me with just about the biggest smile he can muster while I'm doing everything I can not to smack

Zara upside the head. I hand her phone back to her but hang on to it a second to keep her from taking it. "My *wedding*?"

She gives me one of her signature smarmy grins. "Yeah. You know. One day."

"Uh-huh." I finally let go and sit back, turning to Liam. "Send help. I'm going to need it."

"And wine," Zara says. "We'll need that too."

Chapter Four

ZARA and I spend most of the rest of the afternoon doing background investigations into the other two robberies so we can be caught up when we meet with Fairfax police first thing in the morning. I don't see Wallace for the rest of the day, which I'm more than happy about. I don't know what his deal is; he's certainly not like any other boss I've ever had. I'm thinking I might take my concerns to my new FBI-mandated therapist, but right now I'm not sure how much I trust him either.

Eventually the end of the day rolls around and Liam saunters back by to walk me to my car, something he's made a habit of over the past few weeks.

"How was Zara's grunt work?" I ask as we're headed down in the elevator.

"About like you'd expect. A lot of spreadsheets, though," he says. "How'd your prep go? Find anything?"

"Nothing big." The doors open and we head out into the connecting hallway that takes us to the parking garage. "Standard robberies. Thieves are always wearing Santa suits. I don't know if there is a reason or they just have a particular affinity for the holidays. I think if I were going to rob a few places, I'd wear as few identifying clothes as possible. If they hadn't been wearing those suits we might not have tied all three robberies together."

"Criminals never are the smartest, are they?"

"Not really," I reply. "I just want to go home and relax with my dog before the insanity tomorrow."

We pass through the security doors out into the parking garage itself. "You're not looking forward to working the case with Zara?"

"It's not that, I love working with her. It's just all this… holiday stuff. It's not for me."

"Didn't grow up with it?" he asks.

"Actually, no, I did. It was a big part of my childhood. Until Mom…"

"Yeah," he says. "That's how it is for my family too. We're big on the holidays usually. This will be the first year I won't be home for the big day."

I turn to him. "You're not staying here because of me, are you? I don't want to keep you from your family."

"No, nothing like that," he says. "I actually need the break. Things have been…tense with my parents lately. It's better if I don't go. My brother and his family will be there with them, though, so they're good."

"What *are* you planning on doing?" I ask.

"I don't know," he says. "Maybe hang out with you if you'll have me. And don't worry. I won't even mention the C-word."

I smile. "It's fine. It's impossible to escape this time of year anyway. Zara makes sure of that."

"I think she pushes so hard just because she enjoys giving you a hard time."

I spot my car and head in that direction, Liam staying by my side. "She *definitely* does. And don't get any ideas about that picture. I almost killed her for taking it in the first place."

"I never took you for the timid type."

"I can be when I'm not in my element. Which is usually anything other than a suit. Sometimes jeans and a sweatshirt, but only on weekends."

"That's okay," he says. "I've seen the real deal. Who needs a picture?"

"Oh, really?" I ask, arching my eyebrow.

"Yep. Saved and backed up, right here." He presses a finger to the side of his forehead. "Want me to come over? I'd be happy to fix you dinner."

"As appealing as that sounds, I just need to decompress after today. Especially if we're going full steam into this thing tomorrow. Sorry."

"No need to apologize," he says, leaning down and giving me a kiss. It's almost enough to make me change my mind. "What's the saying? Time makes the heart grow fonder? Doesn't matter if it's time apart or together for me. I'll think of you all the same."

Damn he's good. If any other guy were to give me that line, I'd take it as nothing more than a cheap attempt to get me to change my mind. But I can tell Liam is actually sincere. He believes those words with his whole heart. I place my hand on his chest and leave it there for a moment, just feeling the barely perceptible heartbeat beneath it. "See you tomorrow?"

He nods. "If you need anything. Just call. Or text. Or carrier pigeon. I hear those work pretty good, too."

I smile. "Thanks." I reach up and give him another kiss before getting in my car. He stays close until I pull away, before heading back to his car. Liam knows I don't need him to stay around to "protect" me, but the fact he does it all the same is…nice. It's just nice for someone to think of me like that.

Wallace's words have been rattling around in my brain all day, and they might have actually gotten to me if it weren't for Liam and Zara. Having them around makes these kinds of days bearable, especially with an asshole like that for a boss.

I take a deep breath and let my mind wander as I drive back home. It seems like every street is decorated for the holidays. Lights on every street pole or strung between buildings. Each storefront with a different scene, or at the very least, placards proclaiming "last chance deals". The streets are more clogged than normal with shoppers and people running last-minute errands. And starting tomorrow the holiday travel will kick into high gear. People leaving the city to visit family, families coming into the city to visit loved ones. It's a chaotic circus every year. Thankfully, it only lasts a few weeks and then everything is back to normal. This time next month it will be like it never happened at all.

As soon as I get home, Timber almost knocks me over with joy. I give him way too much attention when I come home; I know I do. If I really wanted to train him properly, I would make coming home just a normal activity, but he's always so happy to see me I can't help it. I don't have many people in my life who are *that* excited when I enter a room. So I'm going to milk it for all it's worth.

After taking him out and feeding him dinner, I head to the kitchen and pull out a bottle of hundred-proof bourbon. Knocking one back, I try not to think about what Wallace said today. But it's impossible not to look around this apartment and realize he is exactly right. I can do this job because I don't have any connections holding me down. No family to wake up to on Christmas morning and open presents with. No one fixing a big holiday meal that will test the strength of everyone's belts. No one to fall asleep watching football on the couch with, secure in the fact that no matter what, someone is always there for you.

There are no decorations in my apartment. No indication it's even December. I have a few candles sprinkled about, but they're all still Fall candles. I hate how December cannibalizes fall for winter. While I like winter, it feels like it goes on forever because it starts a full month early. This whole capitalist machine that drives this insanity every year has stolen away my favorite season and I'll be damned if I'm going along with it.

In protest, I head over and light one of my fall candles, though the scent is so weak I don't even know why I bother. I glance over at Timber who is watching me intently and shrug. "Oh well. Worth a shot."

I head back into the kitchen, thinking about where I was this time last year. Matt and I were in our old house, and I have to admit it was more festive than anything I'd done in years. I think he'd finally worn me down and we even had a tree up, though the ornaments were sparse. We didn't do a lot because both our jobs demanded we weren't going to have much time off. Of course he was lying about that the entire time, I just didn't know it until a month ago.

But it had been nice. Just the two of us, leaning on each other, because we didn't have anyone else. I guess I had Zara then too, but we weren't as close as we are now. And as far as I knew, Matt didn't have anyone. The strange thing was I never thought that was weird. I should have. But I guess maybe I felt the same way, so I didn't think it was strange he didn't have anyone else either.

It was a good Christmas. We sat on the couch most of the day, eating leftovers from earlier in the week and watching old movies. Not the Christmas movies they insist on playing all day, but some of the older, rarer stuff, just for something to do. I thought we were happy. But I realize now just how naïve I'd been. Thinking about it now, I still don't know how much of that was real for him, and how much was an act.

I'm not sure I'll ever know.

I down another drink and put the bottle back, then head for the bathroom. I at least need a shower to clear my head. But on the way I pass the envelope that arrived last month. Liam's mention of my mother already put it in my head; I hadn't thought about that envelope for a solid five days until he said something. The envelope with my "mother's" handwriting. I told Liam I would start working on trying to find the culprit, but I don't even know if I should bother. How much of my life do I want to waste looking for someone who is just trying to get a rise out of me? My mother has been dead for almost eighteen years. The only reason I haven't torn it up is I just don't like the idea of someone out there trying to play me.

Still, I ignore it and head back to the bathroom, Timber hot on my heels.

A shower, a quick dinner, and then I'm going to bed.

Tomorrow is going to be hard enough as it is.

Chapter Five

Zara and I walk into the Fairfax Police Department at exactly eight-oh-five am. It only took Zara two minutes to find the station where Sergeant Roeske worked, though I'm not looking forward to our conversation. But because we've already met him, I was hoping we might be able to at least wrangle his cooperation.

After we're buzzed through to the back, we find Roeske without much of a problem. He's in the building's break room, sipping on a cup of coffee as he and another officer are in a heated conversation about a football game last night. The good thing is he doesn't even notice us until we're almost on top of them. As soon as he sees me, he stops his conversation mid-sentence and stands a little straighter. "What are you doing here?"

"Sergeant, good to see you again," I say, making sure my badge is on display this time. "Agent Slate. I'm sure you remember my fellow agent, Zara Foley."

Zara winks at the man.

"Yeah," he replies. "What do you want?"

"You haven't heard?" I ask, feigning shock. "We've been assigned to your robbery case."

"We were hoping you might give us some additional information that wasn't in the file," Zara says, leaning forward so she can whisper a little.

"What the hell?" he says, storming past us. I had hoped we might catch him off guard, but his reaction is worth any blowback. Zara and I follow him through the precinct, only for him to end up in his captain's office. The name on the door says Captain Robert Chisum. He shuts the door as soon as he's inside, not even allowing us to follow him in. After less than ten seconds we can easily make out the shouts coming from within. Zara and I mime looking at our watches as we wait for the tantrum to subside, which it does about five minutes later when the door opens again and Roeske storms out, headed back for the break room.

"Roeske," I call out, causing him to stop and turn. "I'm not going to chase you down. We're here as a *courtesy*."

He seems to consider it for a moment before closing his eyes and taking a deep breath. "Come with me," he finally replies.

We follow him through the precinct to his desk, which sits on the far side of the building, smashed together with a bunch of other desks in a small space. It's cramped and there's only one window, which is closest to Roeske's desk. I'm betting this is his unit, though there's no one else here at the moment. "I'd offer you a seat, but I don't have any." He motions to his desk.

"We don't mind standing," I say. "You've been working the other robbery cases?"

He nods, sitting down at his computer. "Last night was the third in just over two weeks."

"We reviewed the files," Zara says.

"Then what do you want with me?" he demands.

I sit on the edge of the closest desk, across from his. "I want your read on it. What's your theory?"

"There's nothing to read. It's the holidays, people are

desperate and greedy," he replies. "We see more crimes this time of year than any other, surely you know that."

I'm well aware. Another reason not to like this time of year. "But it's not often you see a trio of Santas robbing stores," I say. "Why dress up at all?"

He puts up his hands. "Maybe they enjoy being festive."

"Or maybe they're trying to send a message," I reply.

He looks at me like I'm crazy. "To what end? Don't you think the robberies are message enough?"

"Clearly not," Zara replies. "They have a motive for doing it. Even if it's a stupid one."

He lets out a long breath. "Well, while you sit here and think about how the criminal mind works, I have actual work to do. I'm not about to sit around and wait for these creeps to knock over another store."

"There's another aspect to consider. They're escalating. Why?" I ask.

He nods. "Last night was the first time they attacked anyone. Before that it had been nothing but threats. They just added murder to their rap sheet."

"Did the clerks do something different?" Zara asks. "Anything that might explain the change in behavior?"

He shakes his head. "They tripped the silent alarm, but all three of them have done that." He glares at us. "But thanks to you two, we have a security guard with a concussion in addition to the casualty and assault."

"Thanks to *us*?" I ask.

"If you hadn't chased them down, the security guard might not have been attacked," he replies.

I let out a long breath, steadying myself. "I'm not going to sit here and play the blame game. We don't know what would have happened if we hadn't showed up. But we had a duty to protect and serve, just like you do. What were we supposed to do, let them go? And I'd like to point out, they'd already attacked the clerks by the time we got there."

"Fine, whatever," he says, standing up. "I have witnesses to interview."

"Over at Sibley?" I ask, having already looked up where they'd taken the victims last night. "That's all right. We'll be happy to take care of it."

He glares at me. "You're not taking this case away from me."

"Sergeant," I say, getting back off the desk. "This wasn't my first choice. We rarely work robbery and we're not in the habit of swooping in to take cases from LEOs. But my boss was insistent on us handling this one, and regardless of whether I agree with his assessment or not, I have to follow orders. Agent Foley and I will handle this, but we'll keep you in the loop. Fair?"

He just stares at me a minute before pushing past us, making sure he connects his elbow with mine on his way out.

"Well, that was productive," Zara says as she watches him go.

"Always is," I say. "C'mon. Let's get moving."

We arrive to the hospital a little after nine in the morning, having already spoken with the nurses on duty that the victims are still there for observation. With two head trauma victims, they have to be monitored until there's no more risk from the wounds. While I try not to let Roeske's words get to me, he could be right. The only reason that Santa may have attacked the security officer was because I was so hot on his tail. Otherwise, he might have gotten out of there cleanly, like his buddies.

Then again, I got a different sense from the man. The way he was standing in front of me…it was almost like he was challenging me to come after him. Usually perps aren't like that; they're looking for the quickest exit possible.

Thankfully, because he's not standing in front of the victim's door trying to block our way when we arrive, I'm going to assume Roeske isn't the kind of man who wants to push the issue. That will make things a lot smoother. The last thing I want to worry about is some cop who wants to try and prove something screwing up this investigation. Already we're out of my wheelhouse, we don't need any additional surprises.

"Amy?" I ask, knocking on the door.

"Come in," a weak voice says.

I exchange a quick glance with Zara before we enter. After speaking to the nurse, we found the sales clerk was up on the second floor, in recovery. Amy Watson, age thirty-six. According to her employment history she's been with Ballantyne Jewelers for almost fifteen years.

"Amy, I'm Special Agent Emily Slate, this is Special Agent Zara Foley. We're with the FBI," I say softly. The lights in the room haven't been dimmed, I'm assuming to help keep Amy awake, but I know sometimes it's better to approach victims with a light touch. It's better than barging in here, which I'm sure Roeske would have found completely acceptable. "How are you feeling?"

"Fine, I guess," she replies, touching her forehead where a large bandage covers part of her head and hair. "They had to cut some hair back so they could stitch up the cut. But they said my hair is long enough I should be able to cover it up."

"What's the diagnosis?" I ask.

"He didn't crack my skull, thankfully," she says, lowering her hand again. "Just a deep gash." She pinches her features. "I haven't looked at it yet, can you tell if it's bad? I just don't know if I'll be able to make it go away."

"I'm sure it will heal in time," I say.

"Not by next week," she says. "I'm supposed to be at my parents' for Christmas. I'm sure all they'll be talking about is how strange my hair looks now that it's been cut back." She lets out a long breath. "And no one is going to buy a ring from someone who looks like a five-year-old took a razor to her head."

I exchange another glance with Zara, who eyebrows go up. Amy is understandably having a difficult time after the attack. Anyone in her position would be. We need to handle this as gently as we can. "Can you tell us what happened? We're still searching for the men who attacked you."

She blinks a few times, like she's coming out of a deep thought. "I'm not even sure where they came from. One minute I'm showing this man a pair of earrings for his wife, and the next he's running away and this guy in a Santa suit is standing in front of me."

"How did you know it was a man?" I ask.

"Just looked like he had that kind of frame, you know? The costume was bulky, but I don't know many women that tall. Then I heard Tammi…she just…she screamed and…" She trails off, looking into the distance. "We'd worked together for almost six years. Oh God, her poor mother." Amy's breath hitches and she sobs, holding the bandage on her head.

I shoot a glance to Zara who crosses to the other side of the room, placing a supportive hand on Amy's back. "It's okay," she whispers. Zara has always been better at helping people cope. I never know what the right thing to do or say is. I'm always afraid I'll make it worse. They stay like that for a few minutes while Amy regains control of herself.

"Did any of them say anything?" Zara asks softly.

She shakes her head, though it causes her to wince. "Never said a word. I remember thinking when I first saw him it might be a practical joke, or something the mall was doing…you know, like a stunt to get people away from the big box stores. But I think I also knew something was wrong when I realized he was wearing that mask and sunglasses. First Tammi, then…then they just started smashing the cases."

"How did you get that?" I ask. "By the time we arrived, it looked like you were already bleeding."

She nods. "I was the only one in the front section, and as soon as he started breaking cases I tried to run—I just wanted to get out of there. But as I ran away, he hit me with that club, and I just fell to the ground. I don't even remember much of what happened next. All I do remember is the paramedic shining a light in my eyes."

"Did they go after anyone else?" I ask.

"I don't think so. Everyone else was hiding near the back. And they didn't go back where we keep the safe. Just took the stuff on display."

"What's in the safe?" I ask.

"We keep duplicates of our most popular items back there, along with any special orders or any really high-value items. But there's a time lock on the safe, we have to wait fifteen minutes after putting in the code before it will unlock."

I glance outside, crossing my arms. The sky is growing dark already, even though it's still morning. "Do you think the thieves knew that?"

"Knew what?"

"That they wouldn't be able to get in the safe without waiting the necessary time," I say.

Her bottom lip pouts as she thinks about it. "I'm not sure. How would they?"

"Maybe someone from your company tipped them off," Zara says. "Has Ballantyne been dealing with any disgruntled employees or has anyone been let go lately?"

"Sure," she says. "We lose associates all the time. People change jobs, but I don't think any of them have ever been a problem."

"What's your manager's name?" I ask, pulling out my phone to take some notes.

"Kris Monini. She's the only corporate employee we have."

I pause. "Corporate?"

Amy nods. "Yeah, each store has at least someone from

corporate. If they're not managing, they're checking operations. I know how those guys work; I've been with the company for fifteen years."

"How come you've never gone corporate?" I ask.

She wriggles so she's sitting a little taller. "They say we're required to have a *master's degree*. I barely graduated from high school. This is pretty much the only job I've ever had. And I'm good at it. I don't want to run a store."

"So Ballantyne Jewelers is run by another company?" Zara asks, typing away on her phone as well.

Amy nods. "Rentier Holdings. They own a bunch of smaller stores."

"Including Blakeney Jewelers and Johnson Jewelers," Zara says, putting away her phone.

"The other two stores that were hit," I say. I turn back to Amy. "Who was let go from Ballantyne recently?"

"Wait a second," she says. "You can't be serious. No one who worked for Kris would do this to her. She's a great boss."

"Still, we need to investigate every avenue," I reply.

Amy drops her gaze for a moment. "It wasn't him. I know it."

"Who?"

She looks back up at us. "Josh. Josh Cahill. We…worked together for over five years. But he's not the kind of man who—"

"Why did he leave?" I ask.

"He was fired," she replies. Some anxiousness has crept into her voice. I take a glance at her heart rate monitor and see it has sped up somewhat. "He…sort of went off on a customer. Kris didn't have a choice."

"Went off?" I ask.

"You have to understand, Josh has been under a lot of stress lately." She's sitting up even higher now, her voice more alert than before. "He was just having a bad day."

"What did he do?" Zara asks.

"Just yelled at an older woman who wouldn't listen to him. He was trying to tell her we didn't have any two carat rubies in stock and she wouldn't take no for an answer. If you've never worked retail, you don't know what a zoo it becomes around this time of year. Customers can be *horrible*. And they blame you for everything, even things that you have no control over."

"I can believe that," I say. "Where can we find Josh?"

"You're not going to do anything to him, are you? He didn't touch that lady, he just raised his voice some. But she complained to Kris and Kris told him the policy from corporate said she had to let him go. Some BS about showing the company cared about its customers."

"More than its employees?" Zara asks.

"It's America, isn't it?" Amy says.

I have to concede the point. "Where can we find Josh?" I ask. Amy looks away, not meeting either of our eyes. "We can just get his information from his employee record if we have to. But it would be quicker if you told us. One way or another, we're speaking with him."

She huffs. "Fine. As long as you'll promise to go easy on him. Josh…he can be sensitive." She grabs her phone from the table next to her and scrolls through before turning it to me and showing me the address in her contacts. I copy it down in my own notes app.

"I'll promise we'll listen," I tell her. "But after that, it's up to him."

Chapter Six

"Okay, let's take odds," Zara says. "I'll bet you ten to one this is our guy."

"Ten to one?" I ask as we walk alongside the row houses that make up this part of D.C. It feels like four in the afternoon due to how dark the sky is, but it hasn't opened up yet. And with the temperature hovering around forty degrees, it's going to be a cold rain when it does. "That's a little steep, don't you think?"

After speaking with Amy, we got a statement from the security guard, but he saw nothing more than Zara and I did. We also made a trip down to the morgue to inspect Tammi Rudolph's body. The report was conclusive. She died from head trauma from a blunt object. Likely a club.

"Not for what I have in mind," she replies. "Because if I win, I want to win big."

I narrow my gaze. Whenever Zara talks about betting, I get nervous. Because usually it means I'll have to do something incredibly embarrassing. "How big?"

"How do you feel about going door-to-door singing Christmas carols?"

"I think I'd rather suffer a knife wound," I reply.

"I thought you might say that. So then how about going down to the rescue mission and singing there?"

"Same wound, different knife," I say. "But I *will* go down there and volunteer with you."

"Really?" she asks.

"Sure, why not?" Even though it's a slight gesture, I know the rescue mission appreciates it, especially this time of year. One year for Christmas instead of presents, my parents and I went down to the local mission to work on Christmas day. I think my parents had hoped to instill a sense of community duty in me or something, but I was probably too young to really get it. As I grew older, I saw the value in community service.

Now, it's pretty much all I do. Except now I get paid for it.

"Ten to one odds," I repeat.

"Well not now," she says. "I'll give you five to one. It's only ten to one if you sing."

"And what do I get if I win?" I ask.

"Respect?" she suggests, wincing.

"How about *you* find a present for Liam for me? At least so I don't have to go back to the mall again."

A wicked grin comes across her face. "Oh, I can definitely do that. I think the mall has a Frederick's of Hollywood. A present from there would be sure to—"

"You know what? Never mind," I say. "That's too much power for you to wield."

She busts out laughing as we climb the stairs to the row house and I knock on the door. The metal banisters on each side of the stairs have been wrapped in colored garland and there's a pineapple mounted above the door itself. The box window to our right is also decorated in festive garlands and fruits.

A moment later, the door swings open to reveal a man in his mid-thirties, dressed in a casual suit with a pink undershirt.

He's wearing loafers without socks and is clean cut, sporting what looks like a new haircut. "Josh Cahill?" I ask.

"Yes?" he asks, concern in his voice.

I show him my badge and Zara does the same. "Agents Slate and Foley with the FBI. May we come in? We have some questions for you."

"What does the FBI want with me?" he asks.

"It will only take a minute," I reply.

Thankfully, Cahill seems to decide that he'd rather get this over with than fight us and holds the door open for us. "If you wouldn't mind removing your shoes," he says once we're in the foyer. "I just had the rugs cleaned."

I throw Zara an exasperated look and remove my shoes as she does the same. I realize now Cahill's loafers aren't shoes at all, but slippers with rubber soles. But before I even have my shoes all the way off the scent of orange and nutmeg hits my nose and I catch the sound of instrumental Christmas music coming from somewhere in the home.

"Would you like something to drink? I just made wassail," he offers.

I'm about to refuse but Zara beats me to the punch. "That sounds *amazing*."

"I'm assuming you want them dry," he says. "Unless this is a social call." One look from me tells him he's got it right from the beginning. "I'll be right back." He heads down the hallway beside the stairs, and I notice he's decorated his banister in much the same way as the outside versions, except this one is replete with small ornaments and pieces of fresh fruit.

"Wow," Zara says, looking around. We peek into the main living room which looks out the box window of the front of the row house to find it decorated to the nines. And these aren't gaudy decorations either. Everything matches in color and tone and is done with just enough of a light touch to add warmth to the space without overloading it with décor. Garlands hang above the two doorways, filled with red and gold balls while the bookcase along the far side of the wall has been filled with candles, small glass figurines and books of all kinds. The smell of orange and clove is even stronger in here and there's a gas fire going in the fireplace.

"I'm thinking I should have taken that bet," I tell Zara as we look at all the ornate decorations. It's like this place has been designed by a professional.

"Please, take a seat anywhere," Cahill says, coming back in the room with a small tray. On it are two mugs of steaming liquid, along with a small dish with sugar and a spoon. He sets the tray on the table in the middle of the room before taking a seat in a fancy-looking chair that faces the fire. I notice a book with a bookmark is close by, on a side table.

"Did we interrupt?" I ask.

"I was just taking a minute to catch up on my reading while I still have time," he says, motioning to the book. "Family comes in tomorrow. And then all hell breaks loose."

I take one of the mugs and sit on the couch in front of the table while Zara does the same. The smell from the mug is the source of the smell when we walked in, only much more potent and enhanced by lemon, apple cider and cranberries. I take a small sip, since the mug is still steaming and relish the taste as it coats my throat. As soon as I do, rain begins splattering on the box window.

"Looks like you two made it just in time," Cahill says. "So what can I do for you?"

I set the mug down. "You used to work for Ballantyne Jewelers, is that correct?"

He nods. "I did. For five years. Why?"

"Were you aware they were robbed last night?"

His eyebrows raise in surprise, but other than that there's no change in expression. "I wasn't aware. Was anyone hurt?"

"Unfortunately, an employee died. Tammi Rudolph. Another associate suffered a concussion and is in recovery, Amy Wilson."

This produces a reaction, and he sits forward, his elbows on his knees. "Is she all right?"

"The doctors have her under observation for a concussion and she had some stitches. But other than that, she seems fine."

He covers his mouth with his hand. "Oh, my God. Tammi. Are you sure?"

I nod. "We just came from the hospital."

"She was always such a caring person. And at this time of year…" He's staring off into the distance much in the same way Amy Wilson did. "I can't wrap my head around it. What happened?"

"We're still working on that," I say. "May I ask what's the nature of your relationship with both women?"

"I'm sorry?" he asks, looking at me again.

"Were you friends outside of work?"

He blinks a few times. "Um, sure. I invited them and the others over sometimes, not often. We did a few things outside the mall, but not much."

I motion to the house. "You seem to be doing pretty well for someone on a mall sales clerk salary."

He sits back, crossing one leg over the other. "The truth is, I never needed that job. It was a distraction, especially after… after my partner…died."

For a moment I freeze, finding I'm having a hard time swallowing. "Your…partner?"

He nods. "Donald was…he was my everything. And after he was gone, I felt so…lost. And lonely. I knew if I quit working, it would be that way forever. Out of the two of us, he was the extrovert." He smiles. "He did all the heavy lifting…socialwise. I'm better at the planning side of things." He motions to the surrounding decorations.

"I'm very sorry to hear that," I say, and genuinely mean it. Not only do I feel like we've made the wrong call with Josh here, but I don't feel like we're even in the right zip code. "Did you two work together?"

"He worked for the parent company," Josh says. "But he was still here in town. That's him, in the picture there."

I look up to see a picture of Josh and another man taken in front of a fountain somewhere. Both of them are smiling. Suddenly I can't think of anything but Matt. Of how I felt when he died, and how I threw myself into work. It almost ended up costing me my job.

I think we're barking up the wrong tree here. Why would someone in his position need to knock over jewelry stores? Still, Amy gave us information and we have to follow up on it. I turn to Zara to take the lead because I'm not sure I can do it without my voice cracking.

She picks it up immediately, despite still sipping on her wassail. She swallows quick. "When we met with Amy, she told us you had been fired from Ballantyne."

Josh drops his gaze again. "I guess I shouldn't be surprised she told you."

"Can you tell us what happened?" Zara asks.

"It was just a misunderstanding," he replies. "It had already been a hectic day and it was past closing. All I wanted to do was go home and put my feet up, but we had this one customer who...well, let's just say she didn't like the cut of my jib."

"I'm sorry?" I say.

"She was apparently offended by my lifestyle," he replies. "I always wore very tasteful suits to work, but a trained eye can tell. Some people know what to look for, and others just assume. In the end, it's all the same." He swallows, hard. "I was just trying to tell her we didn't have what she was looking for, but I would be happy to put it on order for her and call her when the stones came in. She kept insisting to talk to someone who...*wasn't queer*...in her particular words. After about ten minutes of that, I'd had it."

"So you told her off," I say.

"Of course the cameras caught it, and Kris fired me the next morning when she came in," he says, deflating in his chair. "I can't really blame her. I was out of line. But some people can just be so—"

"Infuriating?" I ask.

"Exactly. And it's always worse at this time of year."

I nod, then set my mug down and stand back up, satisfied that Josh Cahill isn't our robbery suspect. He obviously cares about his coworkers and wouldn't attack them, not to mention he doesn't seem to have a motive. From what I've seen of this house, he's loaded. "Thank you for taking the time to talk with us. I hope the rest of your holiday is…less stressful." Zara and I head back out to the hallway for our shoes.

"Thank you," he says. "Does Amy have her phone on her? I want to call and make sure she's okay."

"She does," I pause. "And she spoke highly of you. You understand we have to follow every avenue presented to us."

He nods. "Of course. I hope you catch the guy. For Tammi's sake at least."

We give him one final nod and head out into the pouring rain. I was right…it's freezing.

Chapter Seven

"Swing and a miss," Zara says as I get on the interstate. We're both half soaked from running from Cahill's door to our car a block away in the pouring rain.

"Guess I should have taken the bet," I say.

"Maybe next time you'll be smart enough," she replies. "Odds of that guy being our perp are about a million to one."

"I would have loved to get a print of his shoe to compare, but I have to agree. I think we're way off here. He brought up a good point, though. The cameras see everything. Even though they were in masks, we should check the footage. You never know, we might find something."

"We should probably check the footage for the whole mall," she replies. "They were already masked up by the time they got to the jewelry store. But maybe they weren't on their way there. And *someone* had to see them, right?"

"I also want to investigate this Rentier Holdings angle," I say. "All three stores, owned by the same parent company? That can't be a coincidence."

"Let me see if Nadia and Elliott might help," she says. "They can check out Rentier while we work on the cameras."

I hesitate, unsure if I want to give her the go-ahead.

Agents Nadia Kane and Elliott Sandel are recent transplants into our division and despite Zara's assurances they're clean, I'm not sure if I'm ready to fully trust them. Nadia helped us up in Vermont, but it's going to take a lot more than working on one case together to convince me they aren't here just to spy on us. Or more specifically, me.

"C'mon Em," Zara says after I haven't replied for a moment. "I know you don't really trust them yet, but I wouldn't steer you wrong, would I?"

"No, and you were right about them when we needed help in Vermont," I say. "Go ahead, it's fine."

She nods. "Great, I'll text Nadia now. Are we heading back to the mall?"

"Definitely. I want to get a look at those videos before the system erases them."

She finishes her text before shooting me a look and wiggling her eyebrows. "But that means you have to get back in…" She gasps. "…*mall traffic.*"

"Not if we go in the back way," I tell her. She furrows her brow as I switch the radio station to something non-holiday related and floor it. It's times like this when I wish I had a siren and lights in my car.

Thirty minutes later, we pull back into the loading dock area of Arlington Center Mall. Unlike last time, the loading dock is full of activity with trucks coming and going all around us. I find a space off to the side of the main loading areas, but it's tight, even for my car.

"Less busy, huh?" Zara says as we step out of the car.

"C'mon, let's just get this over with," I say and jog across the lot to the loading dock I came out last night. A set of concrete stairs allows us to climb up to the loading area and the doors are already open, despite the fact it's still raining.

Crews are unloading the trucks using extendable conveyors that stretch into the trucks themselves and allow the workers to push the boxes down the line quickly. I show my badge to the dock foreman as we approach and he steps aside, allowing us in. The loading area is a hub of activity, with people moving boxes and pallets around.

I lead Zara around the side to the hallway I was in last night, which takes us back into the corridors. However, instead of turning left, I turn right and head down to the administrative offices for the mall, which are at the far end of the corridor. The offices look almost like a traditional police station, given the glass doors and lack of windows inside. A woman sits behind the desk with a headset on, speaking to someone.

"You check the mall cameras," I tell Zara. "I'm going to find the store's manager and see if I can't get the footage from the store itself."

"On it," she says, heading into the office. I hear her launch into her spiel before the woman at the desk even has a chance to look up. Satisfied Zara will take care of business, I head back down the corridors and make my way out into the mall proper again.

Just like yesterday, it's packed. But not so packed I can't move. At least this time people aren't running for their lives. Thankfully, the local news story last night and again this morning reassured everyone that it was just an ordinary, everyday robbery and that mall security has doubled for the rest of the season. And while I'm grateful for that, I still can't get over the fact none of the perps had firearms. Or if they did, they didn't use them. All I saw were those clubs. Something is definitely going on here. The Santa suits, the weapons, the fact that all three jewelry stores belong to the same conglomerate *and* that one Santa who didn't act like any criminal I'd ever met before all add up to something strange.

As I make my way through the mall, I try not to look at the faces of all the kids or the parents, and instead focus directly ahead of me. That incessant music continues to play its too-happy tunes and it takes all my willpower to block it out. As I'm headed toward the jewelry store, I reach the middle of the mall, where they have set up a giant castle... probably made from cardboard and Styrofoam, though you'd never know from looking at it. It almost reaches up to the glass atrium above. I didn't see this last night; I came out of the back portion of the mall in a different section since we went to the mall offices. But the castle is grand...and somewhat imposing. It sits on a massive plot, with fake snow surrounding it in every direction and lots of plastic or carved animals that have been staged all around, each sporting some kind of winter wear such as scarves or hats and all sporting big smiles. The castle itself has at least three tiers, and there's even a little train running through some of the upper levels, blowing a whistle every few seconds.

And there, at the base of the castle, directly in the center, is a large chair occupied by a man in a jolly red and white suit with a full white beard. He even has on a pair of spectacles. If he were about fifty pounds lighter, I might ask him to step aside for questioning.

Instead, I just drop my gaze and head down the right corridor, back to the jewelry store.

My thoughts are swimming with my parents by the time I reach it, of times when they brought me to the mall as a kid so I could take my turn sitting on Santa's lap and asking for whatever I wanted. And usually, I ended up getting it. Being an only child does have *some* perks after all.

The jewelry store remains closed, and the gates have been pulled down while people work inside, sweeping up the remaining glass. A maintenance team is attempting to disassemble one of the smashed jewelry cases, though it looks as though it's giving them some trouble from all the grunts and groans coming from the men. And there's a cleaning crew working on the carpet where Tammi Rudolph was killed.

"Excuse me," I say, getting their attention by tapping my badge against the metal fence that closes off the store to the mall. "I'm looking for Kris Monini."

"Yeah, hang on," one of the guys says and comes over, lifting the gate. It turns out they haven't locked it; they're just keeping it down to keep anyone out while they work.

"Thanks," I say as he rolls it back down behind me.

"She's in the back offices," the guy says before returning to the others. One crew has cut away the carpet stained with blood while another crew cleans underneath it. As I make my way around another ruined case and step over the man sweeping the glass, I hear a grunt followed by "*dammit*", then a crash and finally a round of groans.

Deciding I don't need to see the carnage, I continue through the back to where the office is located beside a stockroom.

It's sparse, with little to distinguish it, other than the massive floor-to-ceiling safe that sits in the corner. A digital lock on the front glows blue. Beside the safe is a desk with a computer and a woman dressed in a smart suit is on the phone as she glares at the screen.

"Yes, I know what the coverage *says*, but we filed for the endorsement—" She bites her lip as the person on the other side of the phone tells her something she obviously doesn't want to hear. She closes her eyes. "I understand that. But we've—no, that's not the case here! I don't care what it says, you'll have to take it up with corporate. They're the—"

She's cut off again and I swear I can see one of the veins in her forehead bulge. But she keeps it in. "Right. Keep me updated." She doesn't exactly *slam* the phone down, but it's not gentile either. "Fucking snakes." She looks up, only now noticing I'm in the doorway and her eyes go wide. "Oh. Sorry…ummm…?"

I show her my badge. "Special Agent Emily Slate with the FBI. I'm taking over the case for Sergeant Roeske."

She extends her hand and I shake it. "Kris Monini. Does *Roeske* know you're taking over the case?"

I nod. "He does. We had a talk this morning."

She sits back in her seat. "I guess that's why he didn't show up."

"We stopped by to speak with Amy Wilson first," I say. "I'm sorry if you were expecting us earlier."

"No, it's fine. It's not like I'm going anywhere," she replies. "How is Amy? I haven't had a chance to get over to see her yet."

"She's stable, and wide awake, which is what the doctors want, I think," I say.

"That's good. I've already been in contact with Tammi's family. It's such a senseless tragedy. I'm hoping to convince my bosses that we need to provide some financial assistance since she died on company time." Her delivery is cold, though I guess I can't complain she's trying to help the victim's family.

"That's admirable. Unfortunately, Amy couldn't tell us much about what happened. I was hoping to get a look at your security footage to see if anything stands out."

"I've been going over it this morning," she says. "Between phone calls with the insurance agency. They've been dicking me around, telling me our coverage only goes up to twenty-five-thousand and they won't cover anything above that. I've been trying to tell them we have an endorsement that extends that limit tenfold but of course they don't want to hear it." She sighs. "At this point I'm willing to let our lawyers deal with it."

"How much was stolen…approximately?" I ask.

"Only about sixty thousand worth," she replies. "It would have been triple that if they'd gotten in the safe, which thankfully, they didn't. If we can get those cases replaced by the end of the day, I think we can still salvage the season."

"You plan on opening back up?" I ask, attempting to hide my surprise.

"We have to. This is our biggest week. And the week after Christmas is no slouch either. We won't see this kind of traffic again until early February when all the guys are out shopping for Valentine's Day gifts." She pauses. "I'll level with you. We didn't need this. Sales are already down and now we've lost over two days to the dwindling mall traffic. If this keeps up, I doubt we'll even be here next year."

I take the only seat across from her. "Things are that bad, huh?"

She gives me a placating look. "The market is just changing. In all the times I've been working in the business, I've never seen anything like it. Consumers are moving online, or away from jewelry entirely. That foot traffic out there, ten years ago it was double what it is today."

I lean back, noticing how she seems more focused on the business itself than the people running it. "Double?"

"Used to be we could do twenty K on a good day. Now we're lucky to do five," she replies. "But…the market determines where the customers go. And wherever they go, we'll follow."

"When you say *we* you mean…"

"Rentiers. Ballantyne is just a small branch of the business. If it folds, they'll just move me somewhere else. Wouldn't be the first time."

"You have a master's degree, is that right?" I ask.

She nods. "From Wharton. Class of ninety-nine."

"Impressive. Do jewelry stores normally require their managers to carry master's degrees?"

Kris smiles. "Probably not. But Rentier has its standards. Plus, not only do I receive commissions on sales, I also get a bonus based on how well the store does at the end of the year. I was hoping I'd break my record last year when I worked in the automotive division. Jewelry stores typically have higher profit margins. Now…I'm not so sure."

I take notice of the ring on her finger. "Big plans for the holidays?"

"Not really. Just me, my husband and our daughter. Our families live too far away for us to get to them and back in time for our jobs. I'll have to be here bright and early on the twenty-sixth to help manage all the returns we're sure to see."

"I'm sorry to hear that," I say, my heart going out to Kris just a little. "I don't want to take up too much of your time. If you don't mind showing me the footage, I can let you get back to it."

She pinches her features for a moment, then turns back to her screen where she types something before turning the monitor toward me. It shows the store from four high angles, each in black and white. "I've been doing this a long time. Never seen a robbery like this though."

"How so?" I ask, watching the footage. The images on the screens show four customers, each of them being helped by an associate. As far as I can tell, it's a normal day in the jewelry store.

"Usually, the robberies we see are quick grabs. They are in and out faster than we can even hit the alarm. Smash and grab, in and out. But watch these guys." A moment later, I see the three Santas come into view on different pictures. Immediately the customers run out of the store, but the clerks are stuck behind the counters and the Santas threaten them, causing a few to cower on the ground. There's no sound on the video, but I can tell from the aggressive body language they're probably trying to get the clerks to open the cases. I see the main one, the one who faced me down standing in front of Tammi, who has her hands up. They seem to argue and finally he just slams the club down on her head. She goes down in an instant. Then he starts breaking cases and the other two follow suit.

"They're taking their time," Kris says. "Going after the

high-value items only. Why not just grab it all and sort through the stuff later?"

"Because they're inexperienced," I say. "That's the behavior of someone who either has never done this before, or they've been extremely lucky not to have been caught in the past. You're right, it's taking them way too long." Now that I think about it, part of me was surprised to still see them there last night when Zara and I finally reached the store. They'd had plenty of time to get away, and yet they'd stayed to get more goods. Not the actions of a career criminal, or even a smart one.

We continue watching the feeds as Amy tries to run, just like she said, and the one Santa strikes her on the head with the club, sending her to the ground. Less than thirty seconds later, all three of them look up and away from the store. Two take off running in opposite directions, while the third stays where he is. I can't see myself on the screen, but I'm there, staring him down.

Still, I can't see anything on the screen that gives me any indication of who these men are, or anything that might identify them.

"Damn," I whisper as the man finally runs off the screen. I watch as the clerks get up, two of them running over to try and help Amy, while the others go to Tammi. At this point, I'm sprinting after the Santa and he's about to, or already has taken down the security guard. "Is that it?"

"I'm afraid so," she replies. "Not much there."

"No, there really isn't," I reply. I stand and hand her my card. "Can you send me a copy of that footage? We'll want to review it."

"Of course," she says, looking at the card before setting it on her desk. "I'm sorry this wasn't very helpful."

"I've already spoken to Amy about this, but I was curious if you knew of anyone who might have had a grudge against your company or the store in particular?"

She pinches her features. "Honestly, I couldn't tell you. I've been with Rentiers for years, but they move me around a lot. Amy and the others would have a better idea. It's my job to come in and streamline everything."

"No one you fired might have come in looking for some revenge?"

"We offer a generous severance package," she replies. "Rentiers doesn't believe in letting our people go without a little help."

"That's…very generous." I've never heard of retail employees receiving severance packages before.

"Tis the season," she says, smiling.

I stand, preparing to head out. "Thank you for your time. We'll be in touch if we need anything else."

"You'll let me know if you find anything," she says. "The insurance pays out one way or another. If we can recoup the goods, I'll definitely have a better chance of hitting my end-of-year numbers."

Her blatant greed erodes most of the goodwill she'd built with me. Just another symptom of the season. "Sure."

"Thanks," she says. "And happy holidays!"

Chapter Eight

THE ALARM on my phone buzzes and my eyes snap open.

December twenty-second. Two days into what should be a simple robbery case and we're no closer to finding these men than we were when we started. After making no headway with the jewelry store yesterday I caught back up with Zara to go over the shopping mall footage. Again, nothing useful. All three men came into the mall from different entrances and converged on the jewelry store at the same time. It was obviously coordinated. But other than that, we have nothing from the parking areas or anything that might point to their identities.

As I roll over, I recall dreams about following Santas down dark alleyways. But they were no normal Santas, they were clad in gray and white suits, almost like all the color had been drained of them. It was like being in a surrealist painting, though one devoid of any life. And I remember the lead Santa turning to face me, and somehow I was able to see his burning eyes behind those dark glasses.

I rub my eyes a moment before turning to find Timber has crawled up to the head of the bed overnight and curled himself into a ball right on top of the other pillow. It's as if he senses that I'm awake because his eyes open and his head perks up, I'm sure anticipating breakfast.

"Your momma needs to get a life," I tell him, rubbing his head a few times. It isn't often I dream about cases, but I don't enjoy doing it. One of the promises I made to myself was to quit spending so much mental energy on work, though it seems that's still in-process.

As soon as I roll out of bed Timber is down and leading me into the kitchen, looking back every few steps to make sure I remember the way.

"I know, bud. I'm not gonna forget your breakfast. Let's go out first." I pull on a long coat over my sweats and plod out into the cold with Timber on a leash. The temperature dropped overnight, and I have to be careful of the standing water from the rain that might have frozen. He has no problem navigating the stairs and goes to his regular spot. I gingerly make my way down the steps to wait for Timber to do his business, though I find I have to wrap my arms around me, trying to stay warm. But as I wait, my thoughts return to the case.

Nothing on the cameras yesterday. Nothing anywhere. All we have is a partial boot print and with nothing to compare it to, it might as well be a Rorschach. I hate this is taking up so much space in my head, but when I'm assigned a case, I can't help but try to work it out until it's solved. Maybe that's my problem, maybe I have OCD except it's for investigations instead of hygiene habits. Whatever it is, I don't like all these unanswered questions. And without any witnesses or help from the cameras, we need another angle. Some other way to track these guys down.

All the way through breakfast and my morning routine, I'm turning the case over and over in my head. How can I get more information? What am I missing?

As I'm on my way out the door, I give Agent Kane a call against my better judgment.

"This is Kane, go ahead," she answers.

"Hi, Agent Kane, it's Emily…Slate. I was wondering—"

"Emily, how are you?" she asks, her tone airy. "How's the investigation going?"

She's always so bright, even if she is a little shy at times. "That's what I was calling about. Did you and Agent Sandel have any luck with Rentiers?"

"We've been digging, but as far as we can tell, it's little more than a corporate entity designed to buy similar types of businesses and consolidate them. They've bought over sixty jewelry stores in the past fourteen years."

"For what purpose?" I reach my car and slip in, where it's freezing from the overnight temperatures.

"Profit," she says. "They're eliminating redundancies, cutting expenses and increasing revenues. And they're doing it by pooling businesses. They don't just do jewelry stores. Automotive repair shops, tailors, laundromats, all sorts of things. All of them collected into neat little piles."

Corporate consolidation…but on a smaller, more manageable scale. That lines up with what I learned from Kris Monini yesterday. "Can you get me a list of the rest of the jewelry stores under the conglomerate?"

"Sure," she says. "You'll have it in your email in less than five minutes."

I can't help but be kind of impressed. "It's seven thirty in the morning. You don't need to—"

"It's no trouble," she says. "Always happy to help. Let me know if I can do anything else."

I pause after she hangs up, biting my bottom lip. There's something about people who come across as *too* helpful. But on the other hand, that could be nothing more than my paranoia, which Zara has warned me about. Maybe Agent Kane just is that nice.

As I'm on my way to work my phone buzzes with the email. The more I think about it, the more I realize I may have more than I think I do. By the time I get back to the office, I'm reviewing the list on my way up the elevator, checking the location of every store Kane sent me. I'm so distracted that when I come out of the elevator, I almost run smack into Liam.

"Oh! Hey," I say, so startled I almost drop my phone.

"Hey," he says, his voice raspy. One look at him tells me he's been in the office all night, or out on a case. That five o'clock shadow of his is closing in on midnight and his tie is off, the end of it peeking out of one of his jacket pockets.

"Does Wallace have you working graveyard?" I ask. Liam and I are still early in our relationship, at least by my standards. It's really only been about a month and a half, so we're not to the point where we know where each other is all the time. We pass each other frequently enough at work, but given the unpredictable nature of this job, we still have to schedule date nights or anytime we want to get together. It's frustrating, but it's also comforting in some ways because I can sort of prepare for my time with him.

"Stakeout," he croaks. "One of Zara's cases."

Without thinking about it, I place the back of my hand on his forehead. "You're warm. Did you catch something?"

"Probably," he says. "Couldn't leave the car running, so it got a little cold last night."

"Get home, get some rest," I say. "I can drop by a little later with some soup. After I figure out what's going on with this case."

He smiles. "You don't have to do that."

"If I don't do it, who else will?" I say. "Take a hot shower, get under the covers and I'll be by in a few hours."

He pulls his keys out of his pocket and slips one off the ring. "Here. Just in case I'm asleep."

I stare at the key a moment before I realize I'm not saying anything. "Right, thanks," I say, taking it. *I have a key to my boyfriend's apartment.* This is a big deal. Well, it's a big deal for me. He's had a key to my apartment for a few weeks because he had to take care of Timber while I was gone. But him giving one to *me*? It means he trusts me in a way not many people do. Maybe I'm making a big deal out of nothing, but for me it's a huge step forward. "I'll, uhh, I'll see you in a little bit?"

He nods. "Count on it. I'd give you a kiss, but I don't want you to catch whatever this is." He presses the button for the elevator, which opens immediately.

"Yeah, thanks," I say, trying to laugh it off as I realize I'm still holding up the key he's given me. I put it in my pocket, so quickly I almost drop it. *Why am I so nervous? It's just a key!* I wait until he disappears behind the closing doors before I exhale. My heart is pounding. Why was that so intense?

Making my way into the office through our double doors, all thoughts of the list have escaped my mind and all I can think about is if Liam thinks this is as big of a deal as I do. Or was this a more casual thing for him? Did he even realize what he did? I didn't think twice about it when I gave him a key because it was logistically necessary. But…he didn't *need* to do this. He could have just as easily opened the door.

"Hey," Zara walks past, coffee in hand. "What's…going on?" She's eyeing me suspiciously.

"Liam gave me his apartment key," I say, placing the key in the middle of my desk.

"He *what*?" She stares at it.

"Yeah. I mean…it was kind of necessary, I guess. I think he caught something last night and I offered to bring him some soup or something later and he just…whipped it out."

She bites her lip, trying to stifle a laugh.

"Would you grow up," I tell her. "This is a big deal."

"No, you're right," she says, patting my back. "Him whipping it out is a *huge* deal. How huge would you say, though? Like maybe seven…eight in—"

"Z!"

She busts out laughing, almost spilling her coffee. "Okay, okay. Key to the apartment. Serious stuff. What did you say?"

"I think I just kind of stood there like an idiot. I was trying to think about what this means. We now have access to each other's lives. Whenever we want."

"But Liam doesn't just show up," she says. "And I'm sure he knows because you have a key doesn't mean you'll just pop into his place whenever you feel like it. Then again, who knows? Maybe that's what he wants. You might end up catching him in the middle of a shower." She winks.

"Is that what you do with Raoul?"

She gives me a mock grin then heads around to her desk. "You think he's emotionally mature enough to give me a key? Please. I'm always the one who has to arrange anything with the man. He's very focused on his work. If I wanted a key to his place I'd probably have to sign a lease."

"Not going very well?" I ask.

She shrugs. "Still hard to say. But you know me, stubborn. We'll see what happens."

"Still…I'm sorry if he's not living up to your expectations."

Zara takes a sip of her coffee. "That's okay. We have to fail at a lot of things to find the one thing that works, right?"

I nod, picking up the key and slipping it on the few keys on my ring. "Exactly. Which reminds me…the case."

"Right. The *important* stuff." Only someone who knows Zara really well would know she's being facetious. Still, I plow forward regardless.

"I spoke with Agent Kane this morning and she sent me a list of all the jewelry stores that are managed by Rentiers Holdings."

"See? I told you she was cool."

"Uh-huh," I reply. "Anyway, after my discussion with the store manager yesterday, I realized that we're not looking at career criminals here. I think we're dealing with someone with a grudge."

"A grudge? Against the jewelry store?"

"Against the parent company," I say. "They're hitting jewelry stores because it's going to hurt those the most at this time of year. Their other businesses, laundromats, automotive repair shops, and the like, they don't rely on seasonal traffic like a mall jewelry store does. Not to mention their behavior doesn't follow the norms of career criminals. Either they've never done this before, or they are supremely cocky."

"Could be both," she suggests. "So what's the play then? More disgruntled employees."

"No, we don't have time to go through hundreds of employee records. There's no telling how many employees the parent company has. And if Kris Monini is to be believed, they move them around a lot. We need something more direct."

"Like what?" she asks.

"Like if you were a new criminal, looking to offload some ill-gotten gains. Where would you go?"

She pauses, thinking. "You think they'd be stupid enough to try the pawn shops?"

"It's worth a look," I say. "There's over a million dollars' worth of jewels out there floating around. Assuming the thieves aren't just hoarding them like a bunch of dragons, someone has probably heard *something*."

"Okay," she says, nodding. "Then let's try our luck."

Chapter Nine

ZARA and I spend most of the morning scoping out the local pawn shops. While there are tons all over the city, we start with the smallest ones and move up. If I were a new criminal, looking to unload some hot merchandise, I certainly wouldn't start by going to the biggest shops in town. The ones with all the security cameras and that have five-star reviews on Yelp. No, I would start at the smallest, shittiest little pawn shop I could find, hoping the owner might be willing to look the other way when I brought in a couple grand worth of jewelry.

What the criminal probably doesn't know is that most pawn shops report a list of everything they have purchased to the local authorities *every day.*

Not all shop owners do it, but those that want to stay in business do.

Zara and I pulled the sheets for the past few weeks, looking over them for anything that might stand out, but there wasn't much. So my guess is either the criminals didn't use a pawn shop, or they found one who was willing to look in the other direction. Even if they didn't use one locally, these things always have a system to them—a line of back-room communication where they tend to warn each other of impending threats, like local crackdowns.

"Murray," I announce with a big smile on my face as we enter *America Cash Pawn*, which is situated on the southwestern side of the city. It's a small hole-in-the-wall kind of place, no bigger than a couple thousand square feet and shoved between two other businesses, a Korean barbeque place on one side and an accountant on the other. As far as I know, ACP has been here for the better part of two decades, never changing hands.

"Ugh," the man behind the counter says. There's a plexiglass partition which separates the register area so that it's boxed off from the entire store. There's a small slot in the front, big enough to pass bills through, then another drawer to the right which would be to transfer any goods. The room also has a door over on the left side, which allows Murray access to the rest of the store.

As for the man himself, he's heavyset, wearing a white wife-beater, and sports a long beard and very little hair on top of his head. Zara says he resembles a fat Kratos from his mugshot, but I missed her reference.

"Officers," he says, barely looking up.

"Murray, I'm offended," I say. "You don't remember me?"

He finally turns and one eye arches. "Oh. Yeah. Agent Rocks or something."

"Slate," I say. "Emily Slate. And I sure remember you. Almost busted for tax evasion, wasn't it? Skimming off the top?"

He wets his lips with his tongue. "*Almost.* What do I have to do to get you out of my store?"

"We're looking for anything you might have heard about a large quantity of stolen jewelry. Would have been new stuff, straight from retail," Zara says.

Murray leans around me to look at Zara. "Who're you supposed to be? Tinkerbell?"

"That's funny, Mr. Bowman. It'll be even funnier with my foot up to your appendix."

He snorts. "Uh-huh."

"C'mon, Murray," I say, leaning on the shelf on our side of the plexiglass. "We've been all over town this morning. Everyone says you're the man to talk to. You hear about all the deals. Have your fingers in all the pies."

"Funny, haven't heard about that one," he says, his attention back on his screen now, the blue reflected in his eyes.

"Wow," I say, turning to Zara and really pouring it on. "Guess we should just leave then."

"Sounds good to me," Murray replies.

Even though I don't know this guy personally, I know his reputation. In addition to the tax evasion, he's got a rap sheet full of low-level crimes and misdemeanors. I'd guess the only reason he owns this place is because he won it in an illegal bet with someone. Not that this store is the nicest or the cleanest I've ever seen. It's the perfect type of place someone would come to unload stolen goods. There's not even a camera in sight.

But I know better.

"Hey, Z, did you happen to see a report from America Cash Pawn on the sheets this morning?"

"Sure didn't," she replies.

"In fact, I'd be willing to bet if we went back a couple of months, the reports would be sparse, wouldn't you think?"

Murray finally turns to us. "We ain't required to file those."

"But you see how it looks, right?" I ask, getting right up to the glass. "I mean, all your competitors are out there, filing their reports with the police. Building those good relationships, helping each other out. And then there's you. Sitting over here, lonely kid at the table, not sharing his stuff with anyone."

"I haven't broken any laws," he replies.

"Still. I think a little goodwill would go a long way, don't you?"

He glares at me, then at Zara. "No fines. And I don't want any harassment, you got it?"

"Regardless of what you might believe, coming in here was not on the top of my to-do list. I'd rather not be here at all. But I'm what people call obsessive, Murray. And I usually don't let something go until I'm done with it. It's your call."

"Dammit," he mutters under his breath before getting up and heading into the back section of the store. He returns a moment later with a shoebox which he places in the drawer on his side, before sliding it over to us. I pull the shoebox out and open it up to reveal a pile of shiny new jewelry.

"Z." She comes over and begins inspecting the pieces, pulling a glove on before picking any of them up. "Do they match any descriptions of items stolen from the stores?"

"Give me a minute," she says, taking the box over to one of the empty shelves where she begins laying out the pieces of jewelry.

"I guess you have heard after all," I say. "Is that all of it?"

He nods. "Figured it was a lift job. Last time I tried to sell shit like that it ended up almost costing me double. I was gonna keep it for a month before moving it."

"That's very studious of you," I say. "How long have you had it?"

"A couple of weeks. Guy came in here looking to sell it all. Gave him pennies on the dollar and he was happy to take it. We weren't fooling anyone. We both knew where it came from."

"And yet you didn't inform the police," I say. "Despite the fact there had been two high profile robberies at that point."

"Wait, no," he replies. "There was only the one when the guy came in. Second one didn't happen for a few days after that. I expected to see him back in here and I swear I would have called the cops on 'im if he had, but he hasn't been back since."

"Looks like the items match some of what was taken from the first job," Zara says, looking at her phone as she peruses the rings, bracelets, and necklaces. "But this is only about a quarter of what was stolen."

I turn to Murray, scrutinizing him.

"That's all he had, I swear," he says, holding up both hands.

"He might have split it," she adds. "Instead of selling it all to one place."

"Or he could have kept some for later if he wasn't sure about another hit." I turn back to Murray. "We need to see your footage from that day."

"Yeah, yeah," he replies and hits the button beside his chair, causing the back door to buzz. I head around and push through, noting there's a particular odor in here that isn't present out in the rest of the store. "It's back here," he says and I almost have to hold my breath as he passes.

Staying a few feet behind him, I wait for him to reach his security unit, which is a simple monitor with the screen split into four quadrants. Zara is visible on the lower left, still going through the shoebox. Murray types something into the keyboard and the quadrants flip, showing a different time of day.

"December eighth," I say, looking at the timestamp. "That was three days after the first robbery." The time on the screen says nine-fifteen pm.

"Came in right before closing," Murray says. "Anytime they do that I've always got one hand on the shotgun under my desk."

"Registered, I assume," I say.

"Sure, of course."

Somehow, I don't have a lot of confidence in his response. Before I can press him on it, though, the top right camera shows the door opening and a man walking in, carrying the shoebox Zara is holding. He's built differently than I expected, a little shorter and wider than the Santa I squared off with. But he could have been one of the other two. Except I don't have a good view of his face from this angle.

"Is there a better—"

"Yeah, hang on a second," Murray says. The man looks around for a minute, then approaches the front counter. And to his credit, Murray has set up the camera in such a way that there is a clear, unobstructed image of the man's face. It couldn't be easier to identify him.

"I can pull my ledger, but I guarantee he gave a false name," he says. "So all I can give you is the picture."

"I'm glad to know you check IDs here," I say, smiling. Normally I wouldn't be so chipper, but as soon as I saw the face on the monitor, I recognized it. And I think this case has just become a lot easier.

"Look, it's just—"

"Save the excuses." I hand him my card. "Email me that video. And we're confiscating the box of jewelry."

"Big surprise," he calls after me as I head back to the front of the store. "Why don't you just feel free to take all the guns in the case too?"

"I'll be back for those," I tell him, then push through the door back to Zara, who is packing up the jewelry in the box again.

"Sixteen pieces in all. Each one of them from the first job. Approximately seventeen thousand in retail value." She puts the lid back on the box. "Doubt Murray paid a tenth of that."

"Doesn't matter," I say.

"Wait, why are you smiling?" she asks.

"Because I know who our suspect is," I say. "Call it a Christmas miracle."

Chapter Ten

ZARA and I climb the familiar stairs and this time, I'm more than happy to knock as hard and loud as I can. And considering the ruckus coming from inside, I'm glad I do.

A moment later the door opens to reveal a woman in a white shawl, a big smile on her face and a glass of champagne in her hand. There are at least five people behind her, all of them laughing and drinking.

"Hi, come on in," she says, and I can tell she's already tipsy, if not fully drunk.

"We're here to see Josh," I say.

She opens her eyes a little wider and stifles a smile. "I'm sorry?"

We both pull out our badges and show them to her. Immediately, her smile disappears. She elbows the person behind her who is talking to someone further on and they both stop, looking at us. "Find Josh," the woman with the champagne says.

A big man further on down the hallway catches sight of us putting our badges away. "Hey J-man! The feds are here to arrest you!"

The woman at the door hasn't taken her eyes off us, but

she's doing everything she can not to laugh. Yep, definitely drunk.

"I'm here, hang on," comes a voice from the middle of the crowd. Josh Cahill's face appears between two people as he squeezes through them. "Aunt Cheryl, how about you take that back in the living room," he says, cradling the woman who opened the door and physically turning her around so she's facing the other direction. He pulls the door closed behind him and lets out a breath.

"I'm sorry, Agents. My family. They can be…a lot."

I glance over to the box window, so calm and serene yesterday. Today it looks like there is a flash mob in there. "How many family members do you have?"

"It's not just them, it's their significant others, their kids, their friends who didn't have anything else to do. You see why I cherish my alone time before they arrived." He hooks a thumb back behind him. "Did you need to see Amy? She's in there too, doctors released her last night."

"No, we're here to see you," Zara says.

"Has there been a break in the case? Do you know who was behind it?" he asks.

I nod. "We think we do. You lied to us."

His face goes pale. "What?"

"Yesterday when you told us about your partner. You said he was dead."

Josh blinks a few times, then places his hand on the upper part of his chest, near his collar. Much like yesterday, he's wearing a finely tailored three-piece, and I notice his socks have Christmas trees printed all over them. "Donald?"

I pull up the picture I received from Murray on our way over here, showing him the image form the security footage. "If this isn't him, he looks exactly like the man in the picture on your mantle in there."

Josh drops his eyes and his hand. "I…look, it was a particularly bad breakup. I had a lot of difficulty with it, to the point where I was obsessing over him. I just…I thought if I pretended he was dead, it would be easier than admitting that he just didn't want to be with me anymore. That he could have been so…cruel."

"Cruel how?" I ask.

"After he lost his job with Rentiers…his whole demeanor changed. We had been planning a life together, but after that everything seemed to fall apart. He became more distant, and I knew he was lying to me. And then one day, he just…stopped. Wrote me a letter saying he couldn't do it anymore and that if I contacted him again, he would call the police on me and file a restraining order. I was so shocked and devastated I didn't know what to do."

"A restraining order?" Zara asks.

"I know, right? I had never, *ever*, violated his personal space or threatened him in any way. Maybe he saw it different. Maybe he thought there was something to fear, but I know Donald and I think if he hadn't done it that way, he wouldn't have been able to let go. He would have come back, eventually."

"So he cut things off with you…and you haven't heard from him since?"

"I figured if he wanted to reach me, he knew how," Josh replies. "I blocked him on every platform imaginable; I just couldn't stand the thought of accidentally coming across something of his one day. It would have torn me apart all over again."

"But you keep a picture of him on your mantle," I say.

"Agent, like I said, I don't have many people in my life. And I'd rather remember Don as he was, the good times we had, rather than the horrible way it ended."

I feel for the guy, I really do. But he lied to us and has potentially delayed an investigation. "We need to know where he is."

"I don't know," Josh replies. "I think if I did it would be even harder. He probably doesn't even live in D.C. anymore."

"A previous address then," I say.

He looks up. "Wait, you don't think he's responsible for this, do you?"

"Given what you've told us it isn't much of a stretch. People do strange things when they're desperate."

"Not Don," Josh says. "He'd never hurt Amy or Tammi. He knew we worked together. Don wasn't that kind of person."

"An address," I reiterate.

He huffs. "Fine. But I'm telling you, you have the wrong person. He *used* to live at 419 Sycamore, over in Shepherd Park. But that was over five years ago. He certainly doesn't live there anymore."

"How do you know?" I ask.

"Because he lived here for a while…until everything happened. Where he moved from here, I have no idea."

"What's Don's full legal name and date of birth?" I ask.

"Donald George Faustino, named after three of his great grandfathers. And it's August eighth, nineteen-eighty."

That makes him about forty, which matches with the picture. Though Josh is considerably younger, probably still in his early thirties. "Can you tell us anything else about him? What kind of car he drives? Next of kin?"

"He's got parents in Alabama who he doesn't talk to for obvious reasons and a sister in California. That's about it. I don't know what he drives, Don was the kind of man who picked up a different used car every few years."

I close my phone, having jotted down all the relevant information. "It's a start at least. Make sure you don't leave town; we may have more questions for you later."

He motions to the house behind him. "Does it look like I *can* go anywhere?"

"They don't seem to be missing you now," I say. "In fact,

there's so many people in there I'd bet you could be gone for hours and they wouldn't know."

He gives me something of a sneer. "That might be the case if I weren't the one in charge of dinner. Now if you'll excuse me…" He turns and heads back inside without another word.

"Jeez, Em. Kinda harsh," Zara says.

"He lied to us," I say. "He doesn't get a pass."

"Because his heart had been broken," she says as we descend the stairs and head back to the car. "C'mon. You know what that feels like. Cut the guy some slack. Or did your heart shrink two sizes today?"

"No, you're probably right. I'm just frustrated and I shouldn't be taking it out on him. Maybe I'll send him a packet of cookies or something."

"Might want to make that a caseload considering how many people are in that house. So what now? Find Donald Faustino?"

I nod. "Find him, arrest him and interrogate him. And hopefully we can scare him enough that he'll give up his accomplices."

"And then we can get this train back on track and find a gift for Liam!" She pumps her fist in the air.

"Speaking of which," I say. "We have a pit stop to make."

Zara stays in the car, doing a background search on Don Faustino while I stop by a local joint to grab some lunch for Liam. I text him to let him know I'm coming over, but I don't get a text back, which tells me he's probably asleep already. Even though I shouldn't be nervous, I'm cautious about using his key to get in his place. Does he have an alarm system? I can't recall…but would he set it for the middle of the day? Or would he set it at all now that he knows I have a key? All this is so confusing.

"Hello?" I call out as soon as I have the door cracked. "Delivery!"

There's no response. I consider just setting the bag on the nearby counter and leaving, but I figure that would be rude too. "Liam?" I ask but there's still no response. The apartment is dark, no lights are on, but the light from outside is streaming through the windows. The door opens on a hallway, which leads down to the kitchen on the right and the living room slash dining room combo at the far end of the unit. To the left, just past a half bath as you come in the door is another hallway which leads to the two bedrooms. I haven't been over here in a while; usually he comes to my place.

I carefully make my way down the hall and place the food on the counter, wondering if I should put it in his fridge or not. In the corner where the dining room table usually is, Liam has put up a small, five-foot silver Christmas tree with ornaments and ribbons wrapped around it. A glittering star sits on top.

It's not much, but it's cozy. I figure I better at least check on him before I leave. Quietly I make my way down the hallway to the furthest bedroom. The door is cracked and it looks like the curtains have been pulled inside. I push the door open. "Liam?"

"Mmm."

"Hey, I brought you a soup and sandwich from that place you like."

"You didn't have to do that," he says. I still can't see him in the dark, but I know approximately where his bed is. I should, anyway, given how many times we've used it when I've been here.

"How are you feeling?"

"Just tired," he replies. "Here, let me—"

I head in and now that my eyes have adjusted, I can see

him in the bed, covered up. "Oh no you don't," I say, pushing him back down and pulling the covers up to his head. "You need to rest. I'll put it all in the fridge for you, okay?"

"Yeah. Sorry, Em, I'm just—"

"There's nothing to be sorry about. Just take care of yourself. I'll check on you later."

He smiles. "Okay. Thanks."

I have the urge to kiss him, but I have a greater urge not to get sick so I just run my hand along the side of his short hair before getting up and heading for the door.

"Hey Em," he says as I get ready to close it behind me.

"Yeah?"

"Glad the key works."

Chapter Eleven

"How's our boy?" Zara asks as I get back in the car.

"He's still got a fever, but I don't think it's too bad. At least I hope it isn't. But Wallace won't like that he has to give him the time off to recover."

"And since when do we care what Wallace thinks?" she asks.

I give her a quizzical look. "Dr. Foley, I presume?"

"Nah, I just know how you think. And he's not worth the time," she says. "Okay, here's what we got. Donald George Faustino, born August eighth, nineteen-eighty in Winslow, Alabama. Son of Rick and Elaine, sister's name is Kirstie. After the actress, apparently. Who cares? Anyway. Graduated with a bachelor's at the University of Alabama, then went on to get a master's degree from GWU while working in the tech industry. Hired by Rentiers in two-thousand-fifteen, let go twelve months ago due to 'irreconcilable differences', whatever the hell that means. Lives at two-forty-four Baker Street just outside the city limits in Fairfax."

"That's somewhat central to all three robberies so far, isn't it?"

She nods. "And it's not the best part of town. I guess

things hit pretty hard after he lost his job. But that's not the best part."

"What's the best part?" I ask.

She turns the phone to show me. "That would be his wife Judy and their two sons, Marc and Cody."

I stare at the image a second, trying to wrap my head around it. "Uhhh…I'm sorry, what?"

"Yeah, that's what I thought too," she says. "What the fuck, right? Besides his tax records, which show him as married, filing jointly, apparently our friend Donny has another life that I don't think he told Josh Cahill about. He maintained the other address on Sycamore Street in *addition* to the Baker property until about eighteen months ago."

"How could Cahill not know?" I ask.

"Cahill only ever saw him at work, before they got together, right? And he said Don lived with him for a while. My guess is he was leading a double life, playing the part of both husband and boyfriend. Maybe he and his wife separated, maybe he was pulling double duty. His family is conspicuously absent from all his socials. My guess is he leads one life with them, and another without."

"And now he's turned to a life of crime?" I ask. "I guess he would already have the experience to be able to do it without his family knowing. Still. That's quite the find."

"I know," she says. "I'm good, aren't I?"

"So what are the odds Mr. Faustino is going to be home and ready for an interrogation?" I ask.

"I'd say pretty good," she replies. "Considering he doesn't have a job, at least none that I can find. He's been drawing unemployment for the past eight months."

"What about his wife, what does she do?"

"A local librarian, she works for one of the schools in the area."

I wince. Not much money coming in there. No wonder he

started robbing jewelry stores. "Any idea of who the other two perps might have been?"

"Nothing yet. His social media presence is almost exclusively selfies, and from what I can tell he probably went back and deleted any pictures of him and Josh together. There are holes in the timelines."

"He really was ready to end it," I say, thinking. "Do you think his wife found out?"

"There's only one way to know," she says. "I've already put it in on your map. We're about thirty minutes away, given the traffic."

I smile, grateful she's here. I'm luckier than most, and it's times like these when I realize it. "Not bad, Foley. We'll make an honest detective out of you yet."

"Uh, excuse me," she says as we pull away. "I think I just did *all* the work here. I already *am* an honest detective."

"Nah, it's only something that comes with age."

"I'm like eight months younger than you!"

"You'll understand when you're older, trust me." She smacks my arm for good measure, and I can't help but chuckle.

THIRTY MINUTES LATER WHEN WE PULL UP TO DONALD Faustino's house, I see what Zara means about it not being in the best part of town. While it's not exactly dilapidated, it hasn't been kept up, either. The paint is peeling from the siding and the roof looks like it's in need of replacing. The grass is patchy, and I doubt if it will even grow back in the spring. There's a deflated blow-up squirrel dressed in what looks like a Santa outfit on the front lawn that I'm sure will reinflate at night when the small motor kicks back on. Simple Christmas lights decorate the small porch. It was probably a cute house once, but it hasn't seen much care in a long time.

"Wow," Zara says as we approach. "Looks like it might be a slim Christmas for the Faustino family." A blue Ford Taurus sits in the driveway. They have a garage, but from the amount of spiderwebs the door doesn't look like it's been opened in a long time. "So what do we want to do, arrest him on the spot?"

"Pretty much," I tell her. "Just get ready to head around back if he runs. If he's smart, he'll go quietly."

"C'mon," she chides. "How often are they *smart*?"

She makes a good point. Trying to pawn that jewelry was definitely a bone-headed move.

As we get up to the front porch I make sure my badge is on display before I knock. "Hello? Mr. Faustino?"

"There's also that thing right there," Zara whispers, pointing to a small button beside the door. "It's called a doorbell. And you can push it to let people know you're outside."

"Smartass," I whisper back as we hear footsteps on the other side of the door. I tense, preparing myself for anything as the door opens.

It cracks open at first, and I can see the chain is still on the door as a hazel-colored eye peers out at us. "Yes?"

"FBI," I reply. "We're looking for Donald Faustino."

"Don's not here right now," the woman on the other side of the door says. "What did he do?"

I furrow my brow. Given her reaction, I'd say there's about a fifty-fifty chance he's actually in that house. She could be covering for him. "Are you Judy Faustino?"

"Yes." She flits her gaze between me and Zara, and it's obvious she's not giving up any more than she has to.

"May we speak to you a moment?" I ask. "Concerning Donald?"

She seems to consider it before closing the door. I hear the chain off the door and it opens to reveal a short woman, probably no taller than five-two, in a pink bathrobe that's seen better days. Her dark, mousey hair is tussled like she either just woke up or just let it air dry from the shower. She wraps both arms around herself, waiting for us to begin. The door itself is only open about two or three feet, close enough that she could slam the door in our faces if she wanted to. I can tell Mrs. Faustino isn't prepared to let anything go for free. We're going to have to work for this one.

"Do you know when your husband will be back home?" I ask.

"I don't," she replies.

"Any idea where he is?" Zara chimes in.

"No."

I exchange a look with her. "Look, Mrs. Faustino, this is of some urgency. We need to find your husband as soon as possible. We think he may be in danger."

She narrows her gaze. "What kind?"

"I'm not sure. But were you aware two weeks ago he attempted to pawn off a large sum of jewelry?"

Something flashes in her eyes, anger…maybe?

"Do you know what I'm talking about?"

"I know he came home with a lot more cash than he usually carries," she replies. "Don don't usually carry that much money."

"Did he say where he got it?" I ask.

"Didn't ask," she replies. "We had bills to pay so they wouldn't shut off the heat."

I nod. "Have there been any…other times when he's come home with a large sum of money?"

She huffs, pulling herself closer. "He ain't been home in almost two weeks."

"I'm sorry, two *weeks*?" I ask. "Where did he go?"

"Hell if I know," she replies. "Sometimes he just disappears. Eventually comes back around, though."

"What kind of car is he driving?" I ask.

"An old beat-up Chevy Tahoe. Got it from a friend of his a few months ago."

I wait for more, but when it's obvious I'm not going to get it I have to prod her. "Can you tell me what year it is? What color?"

"I dunno, it's black. Two thousand something. I didn't pay attention."

"We know it's not registered in his name, but do you happen to know the plate?"

"Do I look like a computer to you? I barely even saw that piece of trash much less memorized the plate."

"Did you report him missing?" Zara asks.

"No point," she says. "He always shows back up. Just a waste of everyone's time."

I try to catch the woman's gaze but she keeps avoiding me, looking over my shoulder or past me for some reason. "What's the longest he's ever been gone?"

"Maybe twenty days. On a bender or something."

"It's been a while since he's been employed, isn't that right?" I ask.

"He works odd jobs every now and again," she says. "But that don't mean nothing."

Zara glances down at her phone. "What sort of odd jobs? His tax records—"

"These ain't the kinds of jobs that show up on taxes," the woman spits. "Look, I don't—"

"Hey, ma—"

All three of us turn to the new voice behind Mrs. Faustino. It's come from a teenager, maybe sixteen, dark blonde hair with some of his mother's features underneath the acne on his face. He's looking at his phone but stops cold when he sees us, his eyes wide.

"Cody, I'll be there in a minute." She turns back to us.

Cody, Don's son, also happens to be wearing what looks like a light jacket. Now that I think about it, I don't feel any heat from the opening of the door. Seems like their heat might have been shut off anyway.

"Who—"

"They're feds," Mrs. Faustino says, though how she says it gives me the feeling that she doesn't have a very high opinion of law enforcement. That may have something to do with their history, especially if they've ever been threatened to be evicted. It also may explain why she was willing to look the other way when her husband came home with a load of cash.

The boy looks perplexed, almost scared in a way, though I don't have the best view of him over his mother's shoulder. "What—"

"Cody, get back in there. I'll deal with you in a minute," she snaps, causing the kid to immediately turn around and head back the way he came. She addresses us again. "Is there anything else?"

"As a matter of fact, yes. We're going to need your husband's cell phone number. I'm assuming you've tried to call him."

"No point, he never picks up," she replies.

"So you have heard nothing from Donald Faustino in two weeks, don't know where he is, and haven't tried to reach him?" Zara asks, somewhat exasperated. The feeling is mutual.

"Is that against the law?" she asks.

"No, I just figured—"

"If you knew Don, you'd know not to waste your time. Now if you don't mind, what little heat we have left is escaping. I tell you this much, I wish he'd show up again, with another big ball of cash like last time. I'd take it in a heartbeat." She closes the door without waiting for another response from us.

"Well," Zara says, staring at the peeling paint on the door. "That was productive."

Chapter Twelve

I DON'T LIKE any of this. I especially don't like the fact that no one has seen or heard from Donald Faustino in two weeks. Our meeting with Mrs. Faustino didn't leave me with good feelings and her lack of cooperation isn't helping things any. At this point, I'm willing to consider Donald Faustino our primary suspect, given he had possession of the stolen jewelry. We'll need more than that to nail him, of course, but we need to find him first. And the fact he hasn't been home in two weeks *really* bothers me. It's giving me that sick little feeling I get in my stomach sometimes.

"Em," Zara says.

"What?"

"You're speeding again."

I remove my foot from the accelerator and the car slows. "Sorry. I was thinking."

"No, you were brooding. There's a difference."

"Don't you think this is weird as shit?" I ask. "Who disappears for two weeks or more with zero contact?"

"Yeah, something about this is wrong," she says.

I sigh, accepting that we've hit another dead end here. "We need to put out a BOLO on Donald Faustino. And I want someone to keep an eye on their house. I'm still not convinced he wasn't in there."

"You want me to coordinate with the local LEOs?" she asks.

"Yeah, let's see if we get lucky. If he really is in the wind, we're going to have a hard time tracking him down."

She shakes her head. "Why didn't he just get another job? He had to have been more than qualified. I mean, if you lost your job as some corporate shill, wouldn't you just go find another one?"

"You'd think so," I say, agreeing. "It would be better than sitting around your house for twelve months doing nothing."

"But you heard his wife, he's been taking odd jobs," she says.

"And getting paid under the table," I add. "Maybe that's what helped him lead to a life of crime. I wish the wife was more cooperative."

She waits a beat before speaking again. "You didn't bring up Josh Cahill."

"She was already antagonistic enough. I wanted to get as much out of her as possible. Don't worry, we'll take another run at her. But did you get the sense she really doesn't like cops?"

"I'm not sure that woman likes anyone. Including her own kid."

"Yeah," I reply, taking a deep breath. "Merry Christmas, right?" I've never been in the kind of financial straits I suspect the Faustinos are going through right now, but I can't imagine it's easy. It ratchets everything up a few notches, everyone is on hair triggers because you don't know if the lights might get shut off in the next few hours or not. There is no way Mrs. Faustino can support a family of four on a school librarian's salary. She's probably taking out a lot of her frustration on her boys, who will only internalize that pain for years to come.

And it doesn't help things that her husband has been gone for so long.

I turn at the next street, headed back for the beltway. "Do me a favor and check the traffic."

Zara types away on her phone for a minute. "Yeah, avoid the loop. It's a parking lot."

"Great," I say, taking the next right instead. "It's going to take us an hour to get back to HQ on the surface roads."

"It's that time of year," she says, shrugging.

"Next year, remind me to take the three weeks before Christmas off and go to Mexico or something."

"Now *that* sounds like a plan," she replies. "Okay, BOLO is out on Donald Faustino. I sent out his picture and a description of his car as well."

"Hopefully that will at least give us a hit somewhere," I say, thinking. "Where are Rentier's home offices located?"

"Uhh..." she types away on her phone. "Alexandria, it looks like. Office park off Greenway Avenue."

I make a quick U-turn in the middle of the street while there isn't much traffic around. "I want to find out exactly what the problem was with Mr. Faustino. Why he was fired. And maybe we can figure out why he never got another job in the industry."

"Do you really think that will help us find him?" she asks.

"If we can get inside his head, yeah," I say. "We need to get one step ahead of him if we're going to catch him. He's already responsible for one death. I don't want to give him the opportunity to do it again."

"You're thinking about that list of stores Nadia pulled, aren't you?"

I nod. "My guess is Faustino is going to keep hitting stores owned by Rentiers. We should probably coordinate with Sergeant Roeske to get extra security around the stores that haven't been hit yet."

"You really think he's going to do it again? After three clean getaways?" she asks.

"I don't know. But something is driving this man to do these things. And until we understand what happened, we're not going to stop him. Not unless we get lucky. Make sure that BOLO goes out to the jewelry stores as well. I want his face plastered in each of their stores so if Donald Faustino decides to come and case one of the stores, they'll be able to notify us."

"And in the meantime, we get to the real meat of the man," Zara says with a sarcastic enthusiasm. "Why was he fired? What secrets did he know? And now that he's on the run, how do we track him down and stop him for good?"

"You're very funny, you know that?" I ask without an ounce of humor in my voice.

But she just keeps going. "It's late one night and we've tracked him to an abandoned warehouse. Faustino is on the ropes; he knows Emily and Zara are on his tail. He slips on some discarded oil as we near and as we stand over him, preparing to arrest him, he screams out that he's been framed, that this all has been a setup."

I roll my eyes but can't help but smile as I do.

"Pretty good, right?"

"I'd say it's average at best."

"Okay," she says, crossing her arms. "You go."

"What? No, I'll leave the fantasy up to you. I just want to find this guy."

"But you said yourself something about this doesn't feel right. What if he *didn't* steal that stuff and someone made him go into that pawn shop? A *real* criminal would know better."

"You've overthinking it," I tell her. "Donald Faustino is just another guy who made a dumb mistake. That's it."

"If you say so," she says. "But I'm gonna laugh when we walk into Rentiers and find out he was fired for corporate espionage."

~

It takes nearly an hour to get out to the office park where Rentier's corporate is located in Alexandria. The holiday traffic is particularly bad and even though we're not on the interstate, the surface roads aren't much better. After complaining about my taste in music this time of year I finally let her switch the radio to something more festive, but I can only take it for five minutes before I have to shut it off again. She offers to compromise, then connects her phone to the car and begins playing *A Ying Yang Twins Christmas*. I have to admit, it keeps me entertained the rest of the way there.

Finally, we pull up to the building which is nothing special. Just a two-story brick building with a large parking lot half full of cars. It's Wednesday, but we're so close to the holiday I'm surprised to see so many vehicles still in the lot. But more vehicles means there's a better chance someone can answer our questions.

We head into the main atrium of the building, which is a glass section of the building reaching up through both floors and sporting an enormous Christmas tree in the middle. The rest of the atrium is decorated tastefully, including the banisters of two sets of stairs which wrap around each side of the tree. Instrumental holiday music fills the air. Directly in front of us, sitting between us and the tree itself is the reception desk, though I notice the elevators off to our right have a directory listed right beside them.

The young man at the desk wears a headset, but he seems busy working on something as we approach. I clear my throat to get his attention.

He looks up, startled. "Oh, I'm sorry," he says. "We didn't have any appointments on the books today. Can I help you?"

I show him my badge. "Who is responsible for hiring and firing the people who manage the stores under the Rentiers umbrella?"

He seems taken aback at the direct question. "Um…well that would probably be Mrs. Callaway. She's in charge of our personnel department."

"Could we speak with her please?" I ask.

His forehead forms a "V." "Let me see if she's still here. It's our annual holiday party but a lot of upper management has already left for the holiday." He taps his headset. "Cheryl Callaway." Tapping his fingers, he smiles at us as he waits for it to connect. "Oh, Mrs. Callaway, good. There are two FBI agents here at the front desk who would like to speak with you." He covers the end of his microphone. "What's this regarding?"

"An employee who was fired about a year ago," I tell him. He relays the message to the woman on the other end.

"Yes, ma'am. Thank you." He hangs up, then points at the elevators. "You can take those up to the second floor. When you exit, take a left to the end of the hallway and then another left. Her office is the fourth one down. She said the door will be open for you."

"Thanks," I say as we head off.

"Happy Holidays," he calls after us.

"Uh-huh," I mutter as Zara wishes him the same. When we get in the elevator she turns to me.

"No one likes a Grinch."

"His dog seemed to like him just fine," I say.

"Gonna be kind of hard for Timber to like you when I steal him away," she says, ribbing me. "You're just in a bad mood because of the traffic."

"You're right, I am," I say.

"Well try not to take it out on our informant here," she whispers as the doors open and a pair of people get on the elevator as we get off. Both of them have blinking Christmas lights on their necks and are carrying small cups full of ivory-colored liquid. I catch the telltale smell of eggnog as the doors close.

"Christmas party," I say.

"We should definitely crash it," she replies.

"Let's see what Mrs. Callaway says first." I follow the directions the receptionist gave to us until we reach a long hallway of offices, though each has a large picture window that allows us to look into the office as we pass. Most are empty, though one we pass has a couple making out furiously on someone's desk.

"Wow, we never have parties like this," Zara says.

"That's probably a good thing." We find Mrs. Callaway's office, which has her name beside the door and as promised, it's already open. I knock anyway before we stick our heads inside.

"Come in, come in," the woman says, motioning us forward. She's probably in her late fifties, with chestnut hair that comes down just past her shoulders. She's wearing a smart wool sweater and slacks, and I spot a pair of pumps on the ground beside her desk. Unlike her coworkers, I don't see any evidence she's even been to the party. In fact, she seems to be packing things up in her oversized purse. "You're with the FBI?"

I nod, showing her my badge. "I'm Agent Emily Slate, this is Agent Zara Foley."

"You're not here for me, are you?" she asks.

I arch an eyebrow. "Should we be?"

"I hope not," she replies. "I don't know what I could have done. But when someone tells you the FBI is here to see you it kind of gets your heart going, you know?"

"We get that a lot," Zara says.

"We're here to ask you about Donald Faustino. He was an employee about a year—"

"I know who you're talking about." Her entire demeanor has changed and all of a sudden it's like she's on guard. And she's stopped packing.

"He's the suspect in a recent string of robberies that has

ended with the death of a young woman," I tell her. "Can you tell us why he was fired?"

She lets out a half laugh. "Originally? It was because of redundancies. Profits weren't meeting projections, so the board decided to cut unnecessary staff. Said the job of managing our goods division could be done by fewer people. We looked carefully at the qualifications of each individual in the department and decided that Don and a few others could be let go and it would give us a ten to fifteen percent margin improvement in six months."

"Did it?" I ask.

"No," she admits. "We ended up eating the savings in lost revenues. Projections were too aggressive. But had we not let them go, the company would have suffered worse this year anyway."

"How did he take it?" Zara asks.

"At first, it was fine. We told him we'd pay him a severance and help him find alternative employment. But then I found out he'd gone to *my* boss and attempted to get his job back. When I confronted him about it, he became verbally abusive."

"Do you know why?"

"He complained that he'd spent his entire life getting to this point, that he had a lot on his plate and he couldn't just *lose* his job. Yelling how he needed to keep working as the manager at Ballantyne otherwise there would be consequences. He began threatening me."

"Did you file a police report?" I ask.

"No, the higher-ups didn't want the red tape. But we had to hire extra security at the mall so he wouldn't keep showing up, which he tried for a while." She pauses. "I will never forget the look on his face when I told him. It was like his entire world was crashing down. I mean, we offered to help him find another job, but he outright refused, said this was the *only* job he could ever have and that if he lost it, it would destroy his entire life."

I turn to Zara. "Cahill," I say.

She nods.

"What's that?" Callaway asks.

"Mr. Faustino was in a relationship with one of the store employees," I say. "But he broke things off around the same time he was fired. Apparently, he was leading a double life and losing the job meant he could no longer sustain that."

Callaway's shoulders drop. "That explains it. But he never filed anything with HR to my knowledge. If our employees are dating, they're required to let corporate know, especially if it's a relationship between someone in management and a lower-level employee."

"Considering he was hiding the affair from his wife, I'm sure he didn't want anyone else knowing either. Especially his work."

"That's terrible," she says. "Still, he became quite combative. We had to escort him out."

"Would you say he was harboring some resentment toward the company? Rentiers, not Ballantyne Jewelry."

She sets her features. "I'd say that's a definite possibility." She returns to packing things away in her purse.

"I'm assuming you haven't had any contact with him recently. He hasn't showed up here, right?"

"I haven't seen that man since last year and I'd like to keep it that way," she replies. "Was there anything else? I'm anxious to get home. My kids are supposed to be getting our house ready for my husband's parents coming in tomorrow and I doubt they've even started. Not to mention all the cooking that needs to be done."

I hand her my card. "If he happens to contact you or anyone else in the company, let us know immediately."

"I will," she says.

"Happy Holidays," Zara offers as we head out. It's met with a similar sentiment from Callaway. We head back to the elevators. "So? Did that satisfy your curiosity?"

"At least now we know why," I say. "I just hope it helps us find him."

As we head back out to the car my phone buzzes in my pocket. At first, I think it's probably Liam, having finally gotten up. But it's from a number I don't know. "Slate."

"It's Roeske."

"Sergeant?" I say, shooting Zara a look. "Why are you calling?"

"Because I found Donald Faustino."

Chapter Thirteen

"SHIT."

I'm looking down at the washed-out face of Donald Faustino, his milky eyes staring right back at me. He's completely naked, and his skin is so pale it's almost transparent. On the back of his head is a wound similar to the one inflicted on Tammi Rudolph. He's lying on a metal tray at the Fairfax Medical Examiner's office. Sergeant Roeske stands on the other side of the table, his arms crossed.

"Welp. This complicates things," Zara says.

"Let me guess," Roeske says. "Your primary suspect."

"Yeah," I say, somewhat defeated. I expected Faustino to be in the wind, not dead. "How long as he been here?"

"We found him over a week ago," Roeske says.

"Which means he couldn't have committed either of the most recent robberies," Zara says.

"*SHIT!*" I yell, heading over to where the files are kept. I search through them until I find the one on Faustino. It confirms what we could see with our own eyes: death by head trauma and massive hemorrhaging of the brain. "Did you find him, personally?"

"One on my unit did," Roeske says. "I recognized him as

soon as I saw the BOLO. Though when we picked him up he didn't have any ID on him anywhere."

"Where was he found?"

"In an alley next to some garbage cans over on Fremont Street. He was kind of tucked away so you couldn't see him. A homeless guy spotted him as he was going through the cans. Called it in."

"And how long had he been dead when he was found?"

"I think the M.E. said a day. Give or take."

I flip back through the pages of the report. He came in on the thirteenth. Which means he was probably killed on the twelfth. And the second hit was on the fourteenth. "I think your theory is starting to hold more water," I tell Zara. "Faustino may not have been responsible for any of it."

"But he's at least connected in some way," she says.

"Now we just need to figure out who was really behind this the whole time."

"You want us to inform the family?" Roeske asks.

"We've already met the wife, we can do it," I tell him. "But I appreciate the offer." He seems to have mellowed some since our last encounter.

He makes a small motion with his hand. "I've had a few bad breaks on cases in my career too. I know how it goes."

"Thank you," I tell him. "Did someone speak to you about extra security at the other jewelry stores?"

He nods. "I got a call from a chipper woman named Kane. We'll have eyes on all the other locations between now and when the mall closes tomorrow for Christmas Eve."

"We really appreciate that," I say. "Because whoever is behind this, I'm not sure they're done. And if they're escalating, there's no telling how many people might get hurt this time."

He nods, putting his hat back on and tipping it in our direction. "I'll call if anything comes up. Merry Christmas."

"Merry Christmas," I reply without thinking, instead staring at the face of Donald Faustino.

"Emily Slate, did I just hear you wish someone a Merry Christmas?" Zara says, mocking outrage.

"So what?" I ask. "It's not a big deal. We're in real trouble here. We have no suspect and no way to find out who is behind these robberies."

"Unless we just wait for them to go after another jewelry store," she says.

"And the odds of them doing that are about fifty-fifty I'd say. We don't know where the rest of the stolen jewels are, they obviously haven't made their way into any 'official' channels yet otherwise we would know about them." I turn and head out of the morgue.

"Which means they're being sold on the black market," she says.

"Right. If they're being sold at all."

We push through the double doors back outside and head for my car. It's getting late in the afternoon and the sun is already closing in on the horizon. "Who do you want to notify first? The wife or the boyfriend?"

I sigh. Normally we wouldn't inform an ex in a case like this, but I feel bad with what I said to Josh Cahill. He deserves to know what happened to Donald gently rather than just being smacked with the information when it hits the evening news. "Let's go inform Mrs. Faustino first. Then we can let Josh know."

"Talk about a shitty Christmas present," Zara says, getting in the passenger side.

"Tell me about it."

It takes us another hour to get back to the Faustino home. At first I'm worried when I don't see any cars in the driveway, but there are lights on in the home and as predicted, the big squirrel has filled up with air and is now looking bright and overly excited about the nut in his hand as he sits on the Faustino lawn.

"How about I let you do the honors this time?" I offer to Zara as we're approaching the house.

"Why, I'd love to, thank you." As she approaches, she moves toward the doorbell, but then immediately switches and knocks just as hard as I did the first time.

"What the hell?"

She shrugs. "I figure why mess with what works?"

It takes a minute before we hear any movement inside, but eventually the door opens again, revealing a slightly more kept Mrs. Faustino. "You again."

I nod. "Mrs. Faustino, may we come in? We have some news about your husband." I'm watching to gauge her reaction, seeing if perhaps she already knows, but she doesn't reveal a thing. Instead, just stares at us, expecting us to tell her whatever we need to tell her out here.

Finally, either through a battle of wills, or because she thinks it will get rid of us faster, she moves aside, leaving the door open for us. As soon as we enter I can tell the house is only slightly warmer than it is outside. Mrs. Faustino has taken refuge in the living room, where a space heater is hooked up, close to the faux Christmas tree that's been erected in front of the window, though the blinds are drawn.

"Have you read the fire hazard warnings about those?" I ask, pointing to the space heater. "Especially with it being so close to the tree?"

She sighs and goes over, picking it up by the handle and moving it a few feet away until the cord is stretched as far as it's going to go. "You said you had news about Don? What'd you do, find him in the back of some bar, hanging on the arm of some young thing I imagine."

I perk up. "Why do you say that?"

"I might look it, but I'm not stupid," she says. "I know he was messing around there for a while. Must have ended pretty hard when he lost his job, though. Messed him up good. I kind of felt like he deserved that much."

"Did you ever confront him about the affair?" I ask.

"Never needed to. He was torturing himself enough. Figured since it's around the same time as last year it's probably why he hasn't been back. I'm sure he's out there wallowing in self-pity on the anniversary of its death."

Wow. Not that I condone cheating as part of any healthy relationship, but it really seems like these two were not a good fit for each other. "And even though you suspected he was cheating, you stayed?"

"Can't afford to move, can't afford to live on my own. Not with two boys to support. Don don't bring in much, but the unemployment and what little he gets from his odd jobs helps."

"And the occasional ball of cash," I offer.

"Like I told you before, I didn't care," she says. "We needed the money."

"And you have no idea where he got it?" I ask. She doesn't confirm or deny the point. "What about Don's friends? Anyone who might have been someone he'd turn to if he was really hurting for cash?"

"Nah, most of them abandoned him when he lost his job and started the whole 'poor me' routine. People can only listen to that for so long before their ears bleed." She takes a seat on the threadbare couch. "So where'd you find him?"

"Are your sons around?" I ask.

"They're out with their friends, why?"

I take a deep breath. This is always the tricky part. "Because I'm sorry to inform you, but your husband is dead." I watch, closely. And I know Zara is watching too. Looking for anything that might point us in one direction or another or show us that Mrs. Faustino already knows and maybe had some involvement in it.

Her face is like stone for a minute, before she finally winces, like she's been slapped. "No, he's not."

"I'm afraid he is. He was found ten days ago, in an alleyway. He'd been attacked and had bled out. But he didn't have any ID when they found him. We just saw the body not more than an hour ago."

She leans back, sitting against the couch with her hands in her lap, staring at the tree. It's covered in multicolor lights and filled with ornaments, some that look handmade. She's barely reacting at all, but I'm hesitant to make a judgment call on that because everyone grieves in their own way. I will not bemoan someone because they suddenly don't break into tears or start screaming and fall to the floor. However, that doesn't mean I'm still not carefully watching for any signs or signals that she might inadvertently give off.

"What do I do now?" she asks, continuing to stare at the tree.

"Obviously we are looking for his killer," I say. "But we have all the forensic information we need. We can release the body to you for burial or cremation whenever you're ready."

She glances over at me. "Do I look like I can afford a funeral?"

I nod. "If you'd rather, you can come down to the county coroner's office and sign a waiver, which will release the body to Fairfax County. They can then dispose of the remains with no cost to you."

"Fine," she says. "He wasn't worth much in life, I'm not about to spend anything on him in death."

She seems to have regained some of her spitfire after taking in the news. I have no doubt she's capable of breaking this to her children.

"Hey, Em," Zara says, grabbing my attention. I turn to find her pointing down the hallway. I glance around the corner to see the end of the hall leads to what looks like a boy's bedroom, though we can see the closet is wide open and faces the door. Inside the closet is a distinctive red and white suit.

My eyes go wide as I exchange looks with Zara. "Mrs. Faustino, whose room is that at the end of the hall?"

"What?" she asks with a look of disdain on her face.

I point down the hall. "The room at the end of the hall, with the open closet. Who does it belong to?"

"That's Cody's room, why?"

"May we inspect the closet?" I ask.

She gets up, joining us to see what we're looking at. "Why would you want to look in the closet?"

I hesitate, but I'm not about to lie to the woman after informing her about her dead husband. "Because my partner here has noticed a distinctive red and white suit in your son's closet and considering we're looking for culprits wearing a suit much like that, I'd like the chance to examine it, for no other reason than to eliminate your son from the suspect pool."

"Damn cops," she says. "You come in here and tell me my husband is dead and in the next breath you want to invade my son's privacy? Get the hell out of my house."

This is one of those instances where I'm conflicted. I could try to force the issue, but if we found something, it would be thrown out before Cody even saw a lawyer. Still, it gives me pause. What would a teenager be doing with a Santa suit? And given that Cody's father was the one who tried to sell the jewelry, I see that as more than just a coincidence.

We're ushered outside and this time Mrs. Faustino *slams* the door behind us, enough to rattle the frame.

"Z?" I ask, hurrying for the car.

"Already on it," she says, her nose in her phone. "I think I can find him through his socials. Give me a minute."

I pull out my phone and call back into the office. "Agent Sandel speaking."

"It's Agent Slate. Zara said you could assist if something came up."

"That's my job," he states matter-of-factly. "Is it not?"

Boy, he is a weird one. Still, he's a fellow agent. "I need an APB out on a Cody Faustino, age sixteen. Caucasian, dark blonde hair, could be driving a blue Ford Taurus."

"Anything else?" he asks.

"Zara is already looking into his social networks. See if you and Agent Kane can't try to locate the other brother as well. Marc Faustino."

"We're on it and will let you know what we find." He hangs up just as we reach the car.

"Nothing on insta, I'm checking the others," Zara says as she gets into the passenger seat.

"Are you sure about Agent Sandel?" I ask. "He's very…I don't know how to put it."

"Stoic?" she offers.

"That's one way of putting it."

"Don't worry about him, he'll get it done. Now hush, I need to focus. I'm trying to do too many things at once."

I glance back at the house to see the blinds move slightly. I can't see inside, but I'm betting Mrs. Faustino is standing there, watching us from her window. Given everything, I can't really blame her for her reaction. If I were in her position, I might react the same way too. But I can't just ignore the possibility that Cody has some knowledge about what's going on. Maybe that was his father's suit and maybe it has nothing to do with it at all, but we need to find out. It's too big of a clue to overlook.

"Em, you're not going to believe this," Zara says as I pull away from the curb. "I think I found him."

"Where?" I ask.

"Where do you think?"

Chapter Fourteen

As we pull up to the mall, Zara already has Roeske's man inside on the radio.

"He's Caucasian, dark blonde hair, about five-foot seven," she relays to him as we get out of the car. I didn't even bother to park in the lot, instead I pulled the car in the fire lane. Let's just hope there's not an emergency inside, otherwise my car will probably be totaled by a four-ton fire truck. Regardless, we need to be as fast as possible about this. There's no telling if Mrs. Faustino has warned her son. I'm hoping teenagers' general disapproval of their parents will keep him in the dark long enough for us to get him into custody.

"I'll keep an eye out, but there are a ton of people in here today. Sergeant said I was supposed to be looking for people in Santa outfits," the cop on the other end says.

I lean over so I can speak into the radio too. "He may be with a few other individuals. Just keep an eye out for three teens who match the description."

"Ten-four."

The automatic doors slide open as a group of shoppers comes out, toting more bags than they can reasonably carry. This entrance doesn't go through one of the big anchor stores, and instead puts us right in the middle of the action. As soon as we're inside, I realize the cop wasn't kidding. There are a *ton* of people in here.

"Today of all days," I say. "I didn't think teens still hung out at the mall."

"Maybe they do when they're casing a target," Zara says as we join the throngs moving in all directions. I'm not sure where to start, instead I'm just trying to keep a lookout for him.

"I think he had on a gray hoodie and a white t-shirt underneath. And jeans maybe? I just don't know why he would return to the scene of the crime. He hasn't hit any of the others twice."

"Do we even know he's the one responsible?" she asks.

"If it isn't he at least knows something. But a Santa costume in his closet, his dad trying to pawn off the jewelry… all things point in his direction. Maybe not directly, but that's why we need to talk to him. I want to see what he says."

"He's a minor, Em. We can't just interrogate him."

She has a point. I'm used to dealing with legal adults; there's a different set of rules for minors. Though, given his size, it's hard to believe he's only sixteen. And now that I think about it, he's about the same size as the Santa who attacked me. Just another "coincidence" I can't afford to ignore.

As we move through the crowd, keeping a sharp eye, I turn it over and over in my head. How does Cody fit into everything? And why would he be knocking over jewelry stores when his father was the one who was fired? I thought for sure Donald Faustino was our man, but he couldn't have committed the two most recent robberies. And he couldn't have killed Tammi Rudolph.

Zara is doing her best to look through the crowd, but given she's shorter than most people, she can't look over their heads. For that matter, neither can I; I'd need another foot to really see high up. The mall has a second floor, so I motion to

Zara we should head up there for a better look. She nods and we make our way to the nearest escalator.

But just as we're nearing the escalator, I spot him, huddled close with two of his friends. They all seem to be engrossed in their phones, which is good for me. I make a motion to Zara, indicating where they are. She speaks into the radio again, hopefully notifying Roeske's man we have eyes on them and giving him a description of all three of them.

Cody has his back to me and is wearing the same gray hoodie from before. I can even see a few tatters along the sides. Maybe a hand-me-down from his brother, which would make sense. I'm only about fifteen feet away when his head shoots up like a flamingo sensing danger. He scans the area around him and I push forward, trying to get through the crowd before he spots me. But it's too late. We lock eyes and his go wide before he yells something to his friends and takes off running.

"*Dammit,*" I say and start running after him. "Get the other ones! Not like last time!"

"Yeah, right!" Zara yells back and takes off after one of the others while I stay on Cody. This seems remarkably familiar, except this time we're not running through an empty mall and the crowd is slowing both of us down. He slams into people while I'm trying to navigate around them rather than plowing right through them. There are way too many people to try to just bulldoze. Instead, I plot out a direction I think I can run around people, trying to cut some of the distance between us.

He must see my strategy and it causes nothing but panic in his eyes. He bolts forward, knocking a man down before almost falling himself. But unfortunately, it opens up a hole, and he takes advantage of it. I have no choice but to follow, which doesn't give me a chance to check on the man.

He's quick and nimble, vaulting over a row of low occupied couches, and almost knocking the people sitting on them over. I make my way around the couch but it costs me in time. "Stop! FBI!" I yell, holding out my badge so the public doesn't think I'm some kind of crazy person trying to catch this kid. People finally begin to get the hint and part, but this opens another avenue for Cody as well.

Ahead of him I see a larger man drop his shopping bag and move to try to tackle Cody, but he manages to jump out of the way just in time, avoiding the big man. "Thank you anyway!" I yell as I pass. He says something in return but I don't hear it. I really don't want the public involved in this, but if they can slow him down so I can get to him, I wouldn't complain about it.

Ahead of us is the large castle that sits in the middle of the mall, and the area around it is *packed*. All of a sudden Cody finds himself with nowhere to go. He glances back at me, his eyes still wide with terror and he starts shoving people out of the way, trying to get through. It slows him down enough that I finally catch up with him. Instead of slowing down too, I dash forward, tackling the kid and shoving the both of us forward. We tumble together through the small white fence that surrounds the castle and into the field of dressed-up animals before landing right in the center of the platform in front of the castle.

Crap, crap, crap, I think as I work to get Cody's hands behind him and locked in handcuffs.

"What is going on here?" I look up to see a large Santa standing over us, while a small child stands, crying next to his mother.

"Get the fuck off me," Cody yells.

"Sorry, Santa," I say, getting Cody locked down before hauling him up on his feet again. "Official FBI business." He's glaring at me and for a moment I feel like a little kid myself. But I'm not, I'm a trained FBI agent. I smile at the big man. "I guess this one was on the naughty list."

My joke does not go over well as some of the children

behind us start screaming and crying. My face goes red and I escort Cody back the way we came, the crowd parting for us.

"Cody Faustino you are under arrest for the robbery of Ballantyne Jewelers and the murder of Tammi Rudolph," I tell him, reading him the rest of his Miranda rights as we get through the people. As I finish, I spot Zara with a big grin on her face. Beside her is one of the other boys, handcuffed as well. Tears are streaming down his face.

"Glad to see you got him this time," I tell her.

"You too," she replies, though that doesn't explain the grin.

"Did you hear that?" I ask, motioning to the Santa and his elves who are trying to reset the area we destroyed before letting the children back up to the stage area.

"Hear what?" she asks. "C'mon, I think Roeske's man might have snagged the third kid. We need to get them back to the Fairfax police station so we can call their parents or guardians and get this process started."

"You can't do this, I didn't do anything," Cody says.

"He did," the other boy spouts without any prodding from us. "You killed her, man. And you're not even sorry."

"Hey, shut the fuck up!" Cody yells, trying to kick out at his friend.

"Okay, okay," I say, pulling Cody back. "Let's just get you processed."

As Zara and I head to the shopping mall's main offices, we meet up with Roeske's man, who has the third member of our trio in custody. We hold the boys, waiting for backup to arrive to transport them back to the police station.

The entire time the Christmas music playing over the sound system never stops.

Chapter Fifteen

"I AM GOING to sue you for so much the government will run out of money," Mrs. Faustino says, huffing as the officer finishes patting her down and searching her purse as she comes through security. Zara and I are back in the Fairfax Police Department where we've brought all three boys for interrogation. The parents of the other boys, Blake Dryden and Robbie McMarron have already shown up. We've been through the process with both boys already and have just been waiting on Mrs. Faustino and her lawyer before we go in to speak with Cody.

"Mrs. Faustino, please refrain from speaking to the Agents," the man standing beside us says. He's the public defender, assigned to Cody's case since the Faustino's didn't have any formal representation. He turns to us as soon as she's through. "I am going to advise my client not to let her son speak with you."

"That's fine," I reply. "We already have confessions from the other two culprits. Both of them implicate Cody as the mastermind of this whole endeavor. If you don't want to give him the chance to defend himself now, I'm sure it will all come out in court. He'll be tried as an adult, by the way."

"What?" Mrs. Faustino says. "You can't do that."

Her lawyer holds up a hand. "Let me handle this."

"No, I want to speak with my son. He's not to blame here," she says.

"We'd be happy to listen to his side of the story," I say.

Her lawyer must see the indecision in her eyes. "Mrs. Faustino, I strongly suggest—"

"Fine," she says. "I know my son isn't behind this. If you want to talk to him, go right ahead."

"You'll still need to be present, of course," I tell her and I step aside so she can make her way through the station to the interrogation rooms.

"Follow me, please," Zara says.

Mrs. Faustino follows, her head held high, while her lawyer hangs back.

"You better watch yourself, Agent," he says. "One wrong move and I'll get this whole case thrown out."

"Good luck with that," I tell him. As we head through the station, I spot Sergeant Roeske over by the small kitchen. He raises his mug at me and I nod, making a quick detour. As I approach, I drop my voice. "Is he on the way?"

Roeske nods. "Just spoke with him ten minutes ago. Should be any time now."

"Good. Just let me know when he's here."

"Will do. And that's a good collar. Congratulations."

I smirk. "Congratulate me when it's over."

By the time I catch up, everyone is already in the interrogation room, which is really more of a lounge than a traditional interrogation room. There's a couch on one side of the room and a couple of chairs with a small table. Cody is on the couch with his mother right beside him, while the lawyer has taken the seat closest to the couch.

Zara is leaning up against the wall, her arms crossed, watching all three of them. There are three cameras in this room, piping feeds to the officers watching a few doors down.

I take one of the other seats across from the Faustinos and smile.

"Before we begin, I'd like to reiterate that I advise *against* speaking with the FBI on this matter," the lawyer says.

"Do you want to talk to us, Cody? You know you don't have to, right?" I ask, keeping my voice even and emotionless.

I notice his mother give him a little nudge. "No, it's fine," he finally says.

"Let me tell you what we know so far, and you can fill in any holes for us, huh?" I ask without taking my eyes off him. He's staring at the floor, fumbling with his hands. "We know you were behind the most recent robbery at Ballantyne Jewelers. I think you remember that, don't you? It's when you and I first met. We also know you are the one who struck the fatal blow that killed Tammi Rudolph. Which means you're on the hook for murder."

"I didn't mean to!" he yells. "She got in the way; it was an accident."

Mrs. Faustino stares at him like she's seeing a ghost. "Cody, you didn't."

"It was just supposed to be a quick smash and grab," he says. "We needed the money."

"That's not your job," she says and I see the lawyer drop his head, shaking it. "I'm supposed to be responsible for taking care of you and your brother. You aren't supposed to worry about that kind of thing."

"But you couldn't!" he yells. "We don't even have heat, Mom. Pretty soon we won't have anything to eat, either. What are we supposed to do then? It had to be done and I had to be the one to do it."

"But this wasn't the first time, was it, Cody?" I ask. "There was another robbery about a week ago, right?"

He looks away.

"This is all your father's fault," Mrs. Faustino says and for the first time I see her eyes begin to well with tears. It's not surprising. Her entire world is collapsing down around her.

"Why, he's worthless," Cody says.

Her face twists into something resembling rage and she flares her nostrils. "Don't say that about him! He did the best he could. God…I haven't even told you…"

"It's okay," I tell her, watching them both closely. "He already knows." Cody looks up and I finally see the recognition in his eyes, proving my gamble paid off. "Don't you, Cody?"

"What?" Mrs. Faustino asks, placing one hand on her chest. For a second, I think she might hyperventilate.

"Go ahead, tell us about your father, Cody," I say.

"He was cheating on you," he mumbles.

"What?" Mrs. Faustino asks.

"He was cheating on you!" he yells and I see a tear fall from the boy's eye. "I found out he was cheating on you with some rich guy who lives in Capitol Hill."

"Some *guy*? No…" she says. "That…that can't—"

"Unfortunately it's true," I tell her. "Your husband was having an affair with one of his former employees at Ballantyne." I turn back to Cody. "When did you find out?"

"About six weeks ago," he says. "I didn't even mean to. A picture just came up on my feed of them together, one of those suggested posts. I didn't go looking for it."

"And so you confronted him?" I ask.

He nods. "He hadn't been doing anything all year but moping around. We had no money and everything around us was falling apart. And he was just sitting there like a lump! It was his job to help provide for this family, but all he could do was think about himself." He turns to his mother. "That's all he cared about. He didn't care how much he was hurting you or me or Marc. It was always about *him*." There's a vitriol in his words, and I now believe my theory might be true after all.

"You convinced him to do the first robbery, didn't you?" I ask. "It was never his idea."

"It was supposed to fix everything," Cody says. "He already knew the stores from working for Rentiers. I convinced him it would be a good way to get back at them and help the family at the same time."

"And if he didn't, you'd tell your mom about the affair," I say.

He doesn't reply but instead looks away. I glance back at Zara who gives me a supportive nod.

"What happened after that first robbery? We already know your father sold some goods to a local pawn shop."

"Cody!" Mrs. Faustino says. "How did you know how to do all this?"

"I'm not an idiot, Mom," he replies. "I know how the world works." He turns back to me, apparently happy to continue the story. "I knew we wouldn't get a lot for the jewels, so I told dad to split it up and just try to sell some of it, see what we got."

"But you didn't realize that pawn shop owners know stolen goods when they see them. And they pay little when they take on that kind of risk."

"It barely covered the bills for a month," he replies. "We tried to get a better price on the rest, but…things went bad."

"Bad how?" I ask.

"Dad got in contact with some rough people. They just stole the rest and…" He takes a breath. "They killed him." I notice there has been a subtle shift in his body posture. It's miniscule, but it's there. And it's indicative of someone who isn't being completely honest.

"Who did you contact to buy the rest?" I ask.

"Huh?"

"Well, we have to find the people who killed your father," I say. "It would be helpful to know who he was meeting with."

"Oh," he says. "I dunno. He never told me."

"That's not true." He looks up, his eyes wide again.

"What is she talking about, Cody?" Mrs. Faustino asks.

I stare at the boy. "Do you want to tell her? Or would you prefer I do it?"

"T-tell her what?" he asks.

I sit back, straightening. "See, we did a little forensic comparison. And it turns out the wound on Tammi Rudolph's head exactly matches the wound on Donald Faustino's. You said he tried selling the jewels on the black market. But I can pretty much guarantee anyone he'd be meeting would just as soon shoot him as they would have hit him over the head." I pause, watching Cody carefully. His ears have gone red and his breathing has picked up. "But you can't legally buy a handgun here until you're eighteen, can you? Which is why you used the clubs to rob the stores."

"Wait, are you saying that…Cody killed his father?" Mrs. Faustino asks.

"Okay, I think that is enough," the lawyer says, standing. "We're done here."

"What happened Cody? Did he refuse to knock over any more jewelry stores with you? Did that make you angry? Was he just being selfish again?"

"I-it was an accident," he finally says.

"You seem to have a lot of accidents," I say.

"Come on," the lawyer says, motioning for Mrs. Faustino and Cody to get up. "We're leaving. This is nothing but coercion and none of it will hold up in court."

"Maybe not," I say, standing as Mrs. Faustino leads Cody to the door. "But I'm pretty sure when we execute a search warrant for the house, we're going to find the rest of those jewels from the first heist. And the clubs as well. And a shoe that matches a partial of one left the night of the most recent robbery."

"We. Are. Done, understand me, Agent Slate?" He leads them back out of the room, leaving just me and Zara.

"Damn," she says once they're gone. "I thought Mrs. Faustino was going to have a heart attack."

"You and me both," I say, leading us out into the hallway where Cody is being placed in handcuffs again before being led down to the cell blocks. A man in a tailored suit comes up behind us.

"Agent Slate?" I turn. "I'm D.A. Stephenson. Well done in there."

I shake the man's hand. "You were watching?"

He nods. "We all were. We'll be charging Faustino with at least two counts of murder. And he'll be tried as a full adult. There is no way this will go to juvenile court."

"Good," I say. "There's something dark about that kid. I'd be afraid of what might happen if it was given the chance to roam free."

"I guess we all do drastic things when we're up against the wall," he says.

"Yeah. But most of us know when we've gone too far. I don't think he knows the difference. And I'm not sure he ever will."

Chapter Sixteen

"And then Em says, 'I guess this one's on the naughty list!'" Zara and Liam burst out laughing in unison, the two of them cackling with indignity as I sit there, forced to watch as Zara recounts my capture of Cody Faustino.

"Wait, wait, this is too good," Liam says. "She said that to the *Santa*?"

"With a straight face!" Zara says.

"You said you didn't hear anything," I remind her.

She stops laughing long enough to wiggle her eyebrows at me. "I lied."

"Hang on, what did the Santa do?" Liam asks. We're sitting in his apartment, a cup of warm wassail in our hands as Timber snoozes close to Liam's Christmas tree. Thankfully, Liam only had a short bug and was feeling better by the time we got Cody Faustino booked two nights ago.

"He sort of looked at Em like she was crazy," Zara says. "I mean, he was in the middle of having his mind blown, so can you really blame him?"

"Okay, I think that's enough," I say, getting up and heading for the kitchen. "Who needs a refill?"

"No wait, I want to tell it again," Zara says. She rubs Timber behind the ears. His eyes pop open and when he sees me in the kitchen he does a big stretch and joins me, waiting for anything to drop off the counter.

"I'm afraid there isn't time. Aren't your guests supposed to be here soon?"

"Oh, crap," Liam says, jumping up. "I lost track of the time. Can you help me get the appetizers ready?"

"Already on it," I say, refilling my wassail with a healthy dose of bourbon. We went back to see Josh Cahill after the interrogation, to inform him about Donald and ended up staying for dinner. I feel like we mended a fence there, one I never should have broken in the first place. And it must have gone well, because Josh shared his wassail recipe with Zara before we left.

Afterward, we finally managed to get Cody Faustino to confess to everything, but only after the search warrant of his place came up with the physical evidence. They still need to test the clubs we found in his house for any residue that will connect it to Donald Faustino's death, but I am reasonably sure we have our killer in custody. His accomplices have both agreed to testify against him for the murder of Tammi Rudolph if necessary and all the stolen goods have been retrieved and will eventually be returned to the respective stores. As far as I can tell, the only reason Cody went back to the same mall for a second time was because he realized that Josh Cahill used to work there and wanted to hit it again, seeing as their haul from that store was the smallest of all three. Maybe he felt it deserved to be hit twice because it had been the first domino in a line that had eventually torn his family apart. Little did he know it would be the last thing he'd ever do as a free teen.

I really feel for Mrs. Faustino, though. She obviously had no idea what was happening, and now she is left with no husband and one of her sons in jail. I only hope she can lean on her remaining son for support. He eventually showed up at the station yesterday, but I never spoke with him. I think he wanted to see it for himself. That family is going to have a hard time ahead.

Thankfully, Wallace seemed pleased with how quickly Zara and I wrapped this one up. He was even gracious enough to give us the next few days off so we could celebrate together even though more cases keep coming in by the armful. When we go back into the office, we're going to have our work cut out for us.

"Here, we need to keep foil over the canapes," he says. "Once you've done that, they go in for three minutes. I'll get the ham ready."

"Hey, Z," I say. "Foil the canapes for a second. I need Liam."

"Okay, but make it a quickie," she says. "A chef I am not."

"Not for that!" I tell her, pulling Liam out of the kitchen and snatching up a present I'd put under his tree when I arrived last night. We decided to wait until Christmas day to exchange gifts, but I want to make sure he opens this before this apartment fills with people.

I lead him into the bedroom, then hand him the present. "Here."

He grins, taking the present. "What is it?"

"Open it and find out. Zara couldn't quit raving about what a perfect present you'd gotten for me, so I knew it had to be something special."

His grin widens and he rips off the paper, opening the smaller box inside. He crosses his brows as he stares at it a moment, then lifts the garment out of the box. "You got me a dress?"

I nod. "It's the dress Zara made me wear up in Vermont. You said you'd do anything to see me in it."

"Really?" he asks. "Em, you didn't have to."

"I know," I say. "But I don't want to be embarrassed around you. About anything. Plus, this gives you some incentive to make your guests leave this evening. Because afterwards…" I trail off, running my hand down the dress. He takes my face in his hands and kisses me passionately, the two of us getting into it so much I start to think about just locking the door and staying in here for the night.

"Hey! Hurry up, I think there's something burning," Zara says, pounding on the door.

Liam finally pulls away. "Later," he says, breathless.

"Later," I agree.

He heads for the door before turning around. "Oh, wait." Going to his dresser, he opens the top drawer and pulls out an envelope before handing it to me. "You might as well open your present now too."

Confused, I take the envelope and open it. Inside is the business card of a fellow FBI agent. "Who is Agent Dyer?"

"A specialist I met down in Quantico when I was training," he says. "He specializes in handwriting analysis. I know you've been on the fence about the letter from the person pretending to be your mother, but I think he could help. He's the best in the country."

"Oh, wow," I say. "Thank you. You didn't have to do that."

"I know," he says. "But you deserve closure. And you deserve not to have to live with this monkey on your back. He'll be able to help you put a stop to all this. I know it."

"Thank you," I say again, wrapping my arms around his neck.

"Yo, canapes!" Zara says again, rapping on the door. "Hurry it up. A quickie means five minutes or less!"

Liam and I smile at each other. "Too bad you don't have any mistletoe," I say, looking up.

"Don't believe in it," he replies. "I don't need a random flower to have a good Christmas."

"Yeah, neither do I," I say. "This is perfect right here."

Happy Holidays from Emily, Liam, Zara, and Timber!

FREE book offer!
Where did it all go wrong for Emily?

I HOPE YOU ENJOYED *OH WHAT FUN*. IF YOU'D LIKE TO LEARN more about Emily's backstory and what happened in the days following her husband's unfortunate death, including what almost got her kicked out of the FBI, then you're in luck! *Her Last Shot* introduces Emily and tells the story of the case that almost ended her career. Interested? CLICK HERE to get your free copy now!

Not Available Anywhere Else!

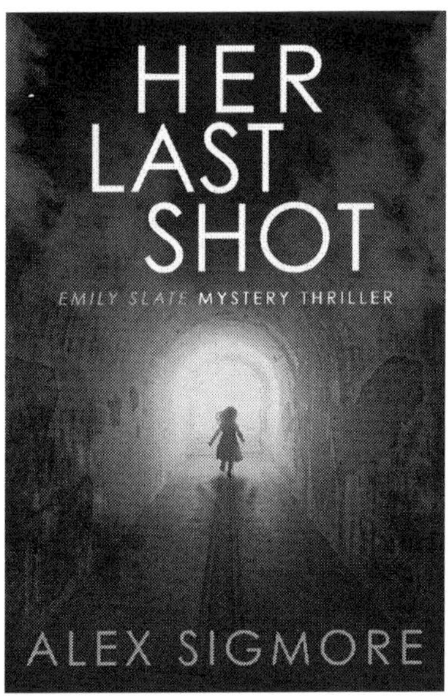

You'll also be the first to know when each book in the Emily Slate series is available!

Download for FREE HERE or scan the code below!

The Emily Slate FBI Mystery Series

Free Prequel - Her Last Shot (Emily Slate Bonus Story)

His Perfect Crime - (Emily Slate Series Book One)

The Collection Girls - (Emily Slate Series Book Two)

Smoke and Ashes - (Emily Slate Series Book Three)

Her Final Words - (Emily Slate Series Book Four)

Can't Miss Her - (Emily Slate Series Book Five)

The Lost Daughter - (Emily Slate Series Book Six)

The Secret Seven - (Emily Slate Series Book Seven)

A Liar's Grave - (Emily Slate Series Book Eight)

Oh What Fun - (Emily Slate Holiday Special)

The Girl in the Wall - (Emily Slate Series Book Nine)

His Final Act - (Emily Slate Series Book Ten)

The Vanishing Eyes - (Emily Slate Series Book Eleven)

Edge of the Woods - (Emily Slate Series Book Twelve)

Ties That Bind - (Emily Slate Series Book Thirteen)

The Missing Bones - (Emily Slate Series Book Fourteen)

Blood in the Sand - (Emily Slate Series Book Fifteen)

Coming soon!

The Passage - (Emily Slate Series Book Sixteen)

The Killing Jar - (Emily Slate Series Book Seventeen)

A Deadly Promise - (Emily Slate Series Book Eighteen)

Solitaire's Song - (Emily Slate Series Book Nineteen)

The Ivy Bishop Mystery Thriller Series

Free Prequel - Bishop's Edge (Ivy Bishop Bonus Story)

Her Dark Secret - (Ivy Bishop Series Book One)

The Girl Without A Clue - (Ivy Bishop Series Book Two)

Coming Soon!

The Buried Faces - (Ivy Bishop Series Book Three)

Her Hidden Lies - (Ivy Bishop Series Book Four)

A Note from Alex

Hi there!

Thanks so much for reading *Oh What Fun*! I love Christmas and I really loved accompanying Emily as she attempted to navigate the holidays in the middle of everything else happening in her life.

I really hope you enjoyed this story and if you would like to see more short fiction about Emily, Zara or any of the other characters, please reach out and let me know! I'm always curious what types of stories you love to read.

As always, please take a moment to leave a review or recommend this series to a fellow book lover. It really helps me as a writer and is the best way to make sure there are plenty more *Emily Slate* books in the future.

As always, thank you for being a loyal reader and happy holidays!

Alex